I Am America

BRAVE BIRD AT
WOUNDED KNEE

A Story of Protest on the
Pine Ridge Indian Reservation

Book design by Jake Slavik
Illustrations by Eric Freeberg

Photographs ©: American Indian Movement/Yanker Poster Collection/Library of Congress, 152; Warren K. Leffler/Library of Congress, 153

Published in the United States by Jolly Fish Press, an imprint of North Star Editions, Inc.

This is a work of fiction. Names, characters, places, and incidents are either the product of the author's imagination or are used fictitiously, and any resemblance to actual persons living or dead, business establishments, events, or locales is entirely coincidental.

Library of Congress Cataloging-in-Publication Data (pending)
978-1-63163-685-1 (paperback)
978-1-63163-684-4 (hardcover)

Jolly Fish Press
North Star Editions, Inc.
2297 Waters Drive
Mendota Heights, MN 55120
www.jollyfishpress.com

Printed in the United States of America

BRAVE BIRD AT WOUNDED KNEE

A Story of Protest on the Pine Ridge Indian Reservation

By Rachel Bithell

Illustrated by Eric Freeberg

Consultant: Royal Lost His Blanket-Stone Jr., Director of
Lakota Studies at Sinte Gleska University

JOLLY
FiSH
PRESS

Mendota Heights, Minnesota

A Note on Names

The people who lived in North America before Europeans came have been called by many names. These include **Indians**, **American Indians**, **Native Americans**, **First Americans**, **Indigenous Peoples**, **First Peoples**, and **First Nations**. This book uses the terms **Native**, **Native American**, and **Indian**, as these terms were used in 1973 by the people who were part of the events described in this book. These terms are still used by many members of Indigenous communities today. However, some Indigenous people object to the terms **Indian** or **American Indian**. **Indian** is rooted in a historical mistake. When Christopher Columbus reached North America, he thought he had landed in India. And the term **American** was coined by European colonizers. They referred to the continent as **America**, after the Italian explorer Amerigo Vespucci.

This book also uses the names of some nations, or tribes. **Lakota** refers to a nation that lived on the plains in the middle of North America. The Oglala are one band within the Lakota Nation. Pine Ridge Indian Reservation in South Dakota is home to the Oglala. Pine Ridge is also the name of the reservation's largest town. In 1973, almost three thousand people lived in the town.

Early French trappers and settlers used the name **Sioux** for the Lakota, Dakota, and Nakota peoples. The word probably comes from an insult used by a neighboring tribe. This book uses **Sioux** only when needed to be historically correct. **Lakota** is more specific and comes from the nation's own language. Most Indigenous people all over the world prefer to use their own names instead of names given by others.

The Apache and Ojibwe nations are also mentioned. **Apache** comes from a word that means "enemy" in the language of the Zuni, a neighboring people. The Apache nation's words for its own people are **Inde** or **Diné**. **Anishinaabe** is the name preferred by the people of the Ojibwe nation. If you ever have a question about what name is best for an individual or group, you should ask them what they prefer.

Chapter 1

February 28, 1973

*P*atsy wanted to go back to sleep, but the pesky buzzer on her clock radio wouldn't let her. She kept the clock on her dresser, out of reach. That way, she had to get out of bed to turn it off. Most mornings, that was enough to get her day going. But this morning, after crossing the room to push the off button, Patsy collapsed back on her bed.

"Pit-a-pat," Mom called, opening Patsy's door. "I've got to go. It's tuna sandwiches in the cafeteria today. If you don't want that, you can take peanut butter and jelly."

Patsy groaned as her mom kissed the top of her head.

"Don't call me Pit-a-pat," Patsy protested. "I'm almost twelve. I'm not a baby."

"As you wish, Miss Patricia Brave Bird Antoine," Mom said with pretend formality. "But you'll always be my baby."

Patsy smiled despite herself. "Speaking of babies, you're going to need some new uniforms soon."

Mom checked the skirt of her nurse's dress, which stretched tightly over her growing belly. Patsy was getting a sibling in about four months. She hoped it would be a girl.

"I think I can alter a few of the ones I have." Mom was always finding ways to save money. "Now I have to get to the hospital. And you have to get ready for school. Dad's in the shower. See you tonight."

Patsy brushed her teeth, combed her long hair, and picked an outfit—a new top with her favorite bell-bottom jeans. By the time she got to the kitchen, Dad was already packing his lunch.

"PB and J, Pats?" he asked, offering her the peanut butter jar.

"Yep." She wouldn't eat tuna sandwiches. She hated mayonnaise.

"You want a ride today?" Dad asked.

The days that Mom worked, Patsy could ride to school with Dad or take her bike. If she got a ride, she had to take the bus home. That added forty minutes to her day. She looked out the window. A bright sun climbed a cloudless sky. Snow covered the mountain peaks on the western horizon, but the sidewalks in her Denver neighborhood were clear.

"Nah, I'll take my bike," she said.

"Bundle up, then. Our winter hasn't given up yet." Dad dropped his sandwich in a brown bag and grabbed his thermos.

"Thečhíȟila," he said on his way out the door. Patsy didn't know many phrases in Lakota, Dad's native language. But she did know that one—"I love you."

Patsy pulled her bike out of the rack in front of her apartment, then donned her gloves, hat, and earmuffs. The two-mile ride to school was chilly. Sixth grade was in the middle school building, not at the elementary school a couple blocks from her house. Middle school had brought some other changes for Patsy. Her parents had decided she was old enough to ride her bike to school and stay home alone after. Her mom used to work just one shift a week, but now she worked full-time. Three days a week, Patsy looked after herself in the afternoons until Dad got home from the garage. Her mom didn't get home until after dinner. Patsy was proud that her parents trusted her. And she knew they were saving the extra money to buy a house, hopefully before the new baby came. Still, sometimes she missed her mom.

Arriving at school, Patsy parked her bike and headed to class. The first subject of the day was social studies. She thumped her textbook down on her desk. She didn't like social studies, and "current events day" was the worst. Once a week, Miss Ashman assigned a student to bring a newspaper article to discuss. Patsy's classmates usually brought whatever was on the front page. That usually meant something about the Vietnam War or the Watergate scandal. Patsy hoped she would never hear another word about either.

Maybe if their discussions accomplished something Patsy would feel different. But her class just went round and round, repeating the same things and getting nowhere.

Was President Nixon a great leader or a thief and liar? Should the United States fight communism all over the world or mind its own business? Miss Ashman was no help. If anyone asked which opinion was right, Miss Ashman just said, "Good question. What do you think?"

The days Patsy had to present the article were the worst. She hated the empty feeling she got in her stomach with all the other kids watching her. And Miss Ashman was sure to ask her a question with no clear answer. Patsy preferred math class. Every problem had one right answer. If she ever got stumped, she could look in the book for a solution.

Patsy's best friend, Laura, slid into the desk in front of her.

"Hi, Patsy," Laura said. "Cute sweater."

"Thanks." Patsy smiled, glancing at the yellow flowers on her top.

"Whose turn is it for current events?" Laura asked.

"It was Carlos last week. Maybe Frank or Donna?"

"I hope it's not Frank," Laura said. "He thinks everyone is secretly a Communist."

Patsy giggled until Miss Ashman clapped her hands to start class.

"Franklin, you're up," Miss Ashman said, nodding to Frank. She never used nicknames. Laura turned so Patsy could see her roll her eyes.

Frank stood at the front of the class to read the newspaper clipping.

THE ROCKY MOUNTAIN REGISTER

——— February 28, 1973 ———

INDIAN PROTESTERS TAKE OVER SOUTH DAKOTA DISTRICT

On February 27, hundreds of members of the Oglala Lakota Tribe met with leaders of the American Indian Movement (AIM). After the meeting, about 200 people caravanned to Wounded Knee, the site of an 1890 massacre. Some members of the group held a memorial service at the grave site of the victims of the massacre. Meanwhile, armed militants in the group quickly took control of the small district. By evening, police and FBI agents had surrounded the area. Protesters and police have exchanged gunfire.

The government is calling the protesters insurgents and insisting they leave the district. The protesters are demanding the land promised in an 1868 treaty. They are also accusing the government of violating their civil rights.

The district of Wounded Knee is located on the Pine Ridge Indian Reservation. It is home to a couple dozen homes, three churches, and a trading post. The trading post, which is owned by a white man, sells snacks and souvenirs to tourists visiting the site of the massacre. Some witnesses say protesters looted the trading post.

At the mention of Pine Ridge Indian Reservation, Patsy gasped. Her father was from Pine Ridge. Her grandma, aunt Marilyn, and cousin Hank still lived there. They didn't have a telephone, so they kept in touch with letters. But Patsy wasn't that keen on writing letters, so she mostly heard news from Dad. If he remembered to tell her.

Patsy hadn't been to Pine Ridge since her grandfather's funeral, more than three years ago. But she was shocked that something like this was happening. With its rolling hills, Pine Ridge had seemed so peaceful.

"An interesting situation, Franklin," Miss Ashman said. "Please, tell us your thoughts."

"I think those Indians better get out of that town," Frank said.

Patsy's stomach felt like it was folding in half. She wondered if any of "those Indians" were her family, and if they were safe.

"Hmm," Miss Ashman said. "Why is that?"

"Well, you can't just go around taking over other people's towns. It's not right. They're probably Communists."

Laura groaned, loudly enough for Miss Ashman to hear.

"Laura," said Miss Ashman, "do you have a different opinion?"

"First of all, the article didn't say anything about Communists. Can we stop it with the Communists? And second, the district is on the Indian reservation. So why does the government care about Indians being in their own district?"

"Well, they shouldn't be looting someone's store," Carlos broke in.

"Why is there even a store there?" asked Laura. "I mean, who sells snacks and souvenirs at a grave site. That's so creepy."

"Good points," Miss Ashman said. "Other thoughts?"

"The article says the Indians want more land, right?" Donna asked. Miss Ashman nodded. "But what would they do with more land? My dad says most Indians are alcoholics who live off welfare. You don't need more land for that."

Patsy's face burned. Was that what everyone thought about Indians? Her dad was a mechanic. Her aunt, like her mom, was a nurse. They weren't alcoholics, and they didn't live off welfare.

"Do you or your father know any Native American people?" Miss Ashman asked, one eyebrow raised.

"Umm, no," Donna said.

"How could she? They all live on reservations, right?" asked Carlos.

"No, Native Americans do not all live on reservations," Miss Ashman said. "In fact, quite a few live right here in the Denver area."

Patsy realized probably none of her classmates, not even Laura, knew her dad was Lakota. It hadn't really come up. Mom, who was white, had chaperoned their field trip to the zoo. But Dad had only been to the school to drop her off. If her friends had noticed him, they'd likely guessed he was Mexican. Lots of Mexican families lived in their neighborhood. There were even a couple families with one parent who was white and one parent who was Mexican. Still, when she was out with both her parents, people sometimes raised their eyebrows or stared. With her brown hair and eyes, sometimes they thought *she* was Mexican. Her skin was lighter than her dad's, but still tan enough that Laura, who had red hair and the complexion to go with it, was jealous.

"Well, time is flying," said Miss Ashman, ending the discussion. "Please open your books to page 124."

Patsy flipped to the page and was relieved to find a map of state capitals. There was nothing confusing or dangerous about state capitals. The students spent the rest of class labeling a mimeographed map of the United States. But when they lined up to go to the art room, Miss Ashman asked her to stay behind.

"Patricia, you seemed a little upset during current events today," Miss Ashman said when the other kids were gone. "Anything bothering you?"

Patsy stared at her sneakers, wondering what she should say. After what her classmates had said, she didn't feel like discussing her family with her teacher.

"Miss Ashman, do you know what the American Indian Movement is?" she finally asked.

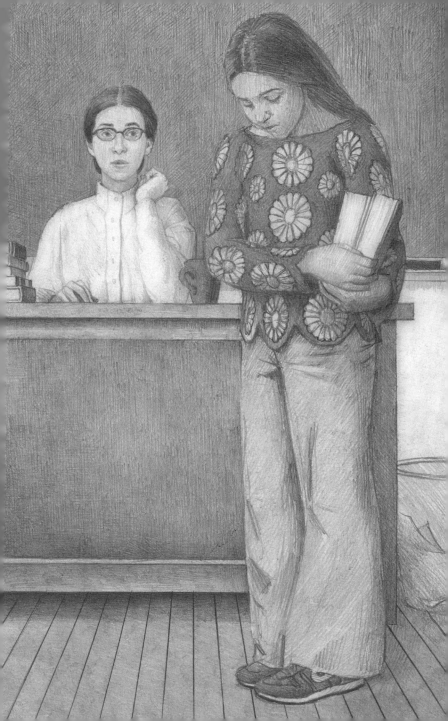

"Just what I've heard in the news. It started a few years ago in Minneapolis. Some of the Ojibwe people there started a group to stand up for their civil rights."

"Civil rights? Like what Dr. Martin Luther King Jr. talked about?" Patsy asked.

"That's right. Like schools, housing, and jobs as good as the ones white people have. And police who will protect them and not pick fights just because they are Native American. Now AIM has spread across the country. People from many tribes have joined AIM. They were part of an occupation on Alcatraz Island a couple years ago. And they occupied the BIA building in Washington, DC, last year."

"Alcatraz? The island that used to be a prison?" Patsy asked.

"Exactly."

"And what is the BIA building?"

"BIA stands for 'Bureau of Indian Affairs.' It's the agency that's in charge of the government's programs related to American Indians."

Patsy nodded but was still worried about her family. "Do you think AIM is dangerous?"

"Some people say they are disorganized and too quick to use violence. Other people say they are brave and visionary. Maybe all of that is true," Miss Ashman said.

Patsy chewed her thumbnail, thinking. "What about that massacre the article mentioned? What happened there?"

"I know many Lakota died, but honestly, I don't remember many of the details," Miss Ashman said. "I am curious to learn, though. It seems like you are too. I'll give you extra credit if you write a report about it. Then we can both find out more. You can turn it in next week. Deal?"

Patsy nodded. She wanted some answers. She might as well get extra credit for finding them.

"You can go on to art now." Miss Ashman waved her hand toward the door.

Patsy had one final question, though—the most important one, in her mind. "Miss Ashman, who do you think is right, the protesters or the government?"

"I don't know enough about it yet to have an opinion, but I wouldn't tell you even if I did. It's not my job to tell you what to think. It's my job to make you think about *why* you think what you think. Now off you go."

Patsy sighed on her way out. She couldn't wait for math class.

That night, for the first time ever, Patsy joined Dad on the living room couch to watch the evening news on TV. The occupation of Wounded Knee was the first story. The reporter said the protesters were holding eleven people hostage, and shots had been fired from both sides.

"Do you think Grandma and Aunt Marilyn and Hank are okay?" Patsy asked Dad.

"I think Marilyn would find a way to get in touch if they were in any trouble." Dad squeezed Patsy's hand. "The women in the Antoine family are smart—and resourceful."

Chapter 2

March 2–3, 1973

"I get two-fifths for problem twenty," Laura said, from her perch on a beanbag. "Is that right?"

Patsy, sitting cross-legged on her bed, checked her notebook. "Yep. Good job."

Laura had come to Patsy's after school to work on homework. She did not share Patsy's love of math, especially fractions.

"Cool beans," Laura said, slamming her book shut. "Now when my mom says, 'Laura Elizabeth, time to finish your homework!' I'll say, 'All done.'"

"Does your mom use your middle name when she's telling you what to do?" Patsy asked.

"Yep, or when I'm in trouble."

"Mine too," Patsy said. "Must be a mom thing."

"What *is* your middle name? I don't think you've ever told me. Is it a secret or something?"

"Not a secret, but kind of unusual. It's Brave Bird."

"Wow, far out. Were your parents hippies?" Laura asked.

Patsy giggled. "No, they weren't hippies. My Dad is Lakota. It's a Lakota name. Or at least it's the English version of a Lakota name."

"Hey, that's the tribe from the newspaper article, about the protesters who took over that district—Wounded Knee!" Laura sat up straight.

"That's right," Patsy said. "My dad grew up outside that district. My grandma and aunt and cousin still live there."

"Is your family okay?" Laura asked, her eyebrows squished together with worry.

Patsy shrugged. "I'm not sure. They don't have a phone, so we're waiting for news. But Dad doesn't think they would have been with the protesters. And I think we would have heard if they were in any trouble."

"So, no news is good news?" Laura asked.

Patsy smiled weakly. "That's what I keep telling myself. I hope it's true."

"Why don't they have a phone?" Laura settled back into the beanbag.

"Umm, I guess on the reservation a lot of the houses still don't have phones or electricity."

"Have you ever been to Wounded Knee?"

"I can't remember for sure. The last time we went to Pine Ridge, I was pretty little," Patsy explained.

Laura *hmm*ed. "What happened at the massacre they talked about in the newspaper article? I know they wouldn't call it a 'massacre' unless a lot of people died, but who died? And how?"

"I'm not sure," Patsy said.

"What about that treaty from the 1800s? What was that about?"

Patsy shrugged again. "I don't know."

"For a girl who is half Lakota, you don't know very much about being Lakota," Laura said, grinning.

"I don't know everything, but I do know some things. I know my dad is proud to be Lakota. So are my aunt and grandma. And our life here is different from theirs, but we're still family. Besides, Laura O'Sullivan," Patsy shot back, "how much do you know about being Irish?"

"Good point." Laura laughed. "But with everything that's going on, aren't you curious about some of the things you don't know?"

"Yep," Patsy said. "I am curious. And I plan to find some answers. Miss Ashman said she'd give me extra credit to write a report about the massacre. I'm going to the library tomorrow."

"That's good, because you could use some extra credit in social studies," Laura teased. Patsy threw her pillow at her best friend. Laura easily caught it and lobbed it back.

"Seriously, though," Laura said, "why didn't you say anything in class about your family being from Pine Ridge?"

Patsy chewed her thumbnail. "Well, you heard the mean things Frank and Donna said. And people would have questions, like you did. I've never lived on the reservation. I can't speak for all Lakota people, much less all Native people. And I don't know what to think about AIM and this occupation yet. Even Miss Ashman couldn't say who was right and who was wrong. How am I supposed to figure it out?"

"I get that," Laura said. "I won't say anything about it unless you want me to."

~

The next morning, Mom and Dad were putting together a baby crib when Patsy went looking for them.

"Isn't it kind of early to put up the crib?" she asked.

"One of the receptionists at the hospital gave it to us," Mom said. "Her little boy outgrew it. Since it's secondhand, we want to be sure all the parts are here."

"What if something's missing?"

"Then Dad will fix it. He can fix anything," Mom said, with a wink. "Anyway, what's up, Pit-a-pat?"

"Don't call me that," Patsy said. "Can I go to the library?"

"On a Saturday morning?" Dad asked skeptically.

"Yeah, Miss Ashman offered me extra credit to write a report about the Wounded Knee Massacre, and there's nothing about it in my history book."

"That's not surprising," said Dad. "I'm not sure how much you'll find at the library either."

"Why?" Patsy asked.

"Because history books get written by white people, and a lot of white people don't want to talk about Wounded Knee."

"But then how will I write my report?" Patsy asked, worried.

"Tell you what," Dad said, "why don't you go see what you can find at the library. Then show me your report, and I'll help you fill in what's missing."

A half hour later, Patsy pulled the W volume of the encyclopedia off the library shelf. There was no entry for "Wounded Knee." Next, she tried the card catalog. She had to look through half a dozen subjects and ask a librarian for help, but finally she found what she needed. Two books, called *Bury My Heart at Wounded Knee* and *Black Elk Speaks*, had chapters about the massacre. She left the library a couple hours later with her report neatly written in her notebook.

The Wounded Knee Massacre of 1890
By Patsy Antoine

In the 1850s and 1860s, many white settlers entered the territory of the Lakota people. Conflicts between them became more common and more deadly. In 1868, the US government and some Lakota chiefs agreed to the Treaty of Fort Laramie, which formed the Great Sioux Reservation. It included the western half of what is now South Dakota and parts of Nebraska and Montana.

The treaty said the reservation was for use by the Lakota people only. But in the early 1870s, gold was discovered on the reservation. Miners and prospectors streamed in. Instead of enforcing the treaty, the US government sent the army to help the white settlers. The Lakota fought back. In 1876, the Lakota and some allies defeated Lieutenant Colonel George Custer and the Seventh Cavalry at the Battle of the Little Bighorn.

The US government retaliated by sending more troops into Lakota territory. They also sent hunters to wipe out the herds of buffalo the Lakota depended on for food, shelter, and clothing. In 1889, Congress cut the size of the Great Sioux Reservation almost in half. What was left was divided into five small reservations. Feeling desperate, many Lakota found hope in a religion called the Ghost Dance. It taught that a savior was soon coming to return Native lands to Native people and bring back many of their ancestors.

In 1890, many Lakota were gathering to perform the Ghost Dance, including some followers of Chief Sitting Bull. The US government feared the popular chief would gather more power. The army sent dozens of police to Standing Rock Reservation to arrest him on December 15, 1890. These police were Native men hired by the Office of Indian Affairs. During the attempt, the police shot and killed Sitting Bull. Fearing more violence in the area, Chief Spotted Elk fled with a band of about 350 people. Most were women, children, or elderly. They headed for the Pine Ridge Indian Reservation to join Chief

Red Cloud and his people, but they never got there. On December 28, 1890, the Seventh Cavalry intercepted them. The US soldiers forced Spotted Elk and his people to camp near Wounded Knee Creek.

During the night, the soldiers surrounded the camp and set up four small cannons. In the morning, the soldiers separated the Lakota men from the women and children. Then they ordered the men to give up their weapons. The Lakota stacked their guns as ordered, but the soldiers were afraid they might be hiding some weapons. The soldiers searched the tipis and the men. During the search, a shot rang out. No one is sure who fired it, but the army didn't wait to find out. They opened fire with guns and cannon. Between 150 and 300 Lakota died. More than half were women and children. Soldiers chased down and shot many of them as they were hiding or running away.

A blizzard blew in, and the dead were left outside for several days. They were finally buried a week later in a mass grave. The grieving Lakota marked the site with prayer sticks. Finally, in 1903, the Lakota placed a permanent monument to mark the grave.

When Patsy arrived at home, the crib was complete, taking up half their small living room.

"Don't worry," Mom said. "We'll take it down again this afternoon. But isn't it cute? And we have all the pieces."

Patsy tried to return her mother's smile but couldn't seem to make her cheeks work the right way.

"What's wrong?" Mom asked.

"I just spent the morning reading about the Wounded Knee Massacre," Patsy said. "It was awful. The army shot old people and children, even little babies."

"It was awful," Dad agreed. "Do you want to talk about it?"

"I thought it was probably a battle where a lot of people got killed," Patsy said. "But the Lakota had already given up their weapons when the army started shooting. The soldiers were killing defenseless people."

"I know," Dad said. "And the Lakota were hungry and freezing. Chief Spotted Elk was so sick with pneumonia he couldn't even get up. They shot him in his bed. Did you know that twenty soldiers got medals of honor for their bravery at Wounded Knee? I just can't see how anyone thought what they did took any honor or bravery." Dad shook his head. "Can I read your report?"

Patsy handed her notebook to Dad. Mom read over his shoulder.

"You found some good accounts," Dad said. "Books that were honest about what happened."

"Have you ever been to Wounded Knee and seen the monument?" Patsy asked.

"We all have," Dad said. "It's just a few miles from the house I grew up in, where your grandmother and aunt live. We took you there once, but I'm not surprised you don't remember. You were pretty young."

"I want to go back someday," Patsy said. "So I can remember it."

Dad handed the notebook back to her and put an arm around her shoulder. "I'd like that too."

Chapter 3

March 5, 1973

"Let's check the mail on the way in," Mom said as she parked the car. She and Patsy had stopped at the grocery store after school. They were anxious for a letter from Aunt Marilyn.

The row of mailboxes for the four apartments in their building stood beside the parking lot. With bags of groceries in both arms, Mom fumbled to get the key from her pocket. She passed it to Patsy, who had a free hand.

The little lock clicked, and the door swung open to reveal—nothing. The mail hadn't arrived yet.

Mom sighed. "Looks like the mail carrier is running late. We can check again after dinner."

Inside their apartment, Mom put Patsy to work chopping vegetables for a salad while she made spaghetti sauce. As she sliced carrots, Patsy thought about her South Dakota relatives.

"Mom, isn't it kind of funny that you and Aunt Marilyn are both nurses?" she said.

"It's not exactly a coincidence," Mom said. "That's how we met. The first day of nursing school, I got to class early. I found a desk and piled up all my shiny new textbooks. A tall girl with a black ponytail sat at the desk next to me. She watched me fiddling with my books for a minute. Then she said, 'Do you think we really need all those? 'Cause they're not cheap.' We were both so nervous, we burst out laughing."

"And that girl was Aunt Marilyn?" Patsy guessed.

"Exactly," Mom said. "After that, we sat by each other every day. We shared the books—to save money. Pretty soon, I started coming to her apartment to study. And she lived with her tall, dark, and handsome older brother."

"And that was Dad?"

"You got it." Mom smiled as she stirred tomato sauce. "Your dad was quiet but funny and charming. And his sister adored him, which says a lot for a guy, if you ask me."

"How did Dad and Aunt Marilyn get to Denver if they grew up in South Dakota?"

"Dad came first, to go to school. During the '50s and '60s the government was offering young people on reservations money to move to cities. They could go to school or get jobs. It was called the Indian Relocation Program. Your dad got a bus ticket, and they paid tuition for him to train as a mechanic."

"So that's why he became a mechanic, because the government paid for his school?"

"He already knew how to fix cars," Mom said. "He'd learned from his dad. And his dad learned while he was in the army. But your dad needed a piece of paper that proved he knew how to fix cars to get a job. After that, he stayed and worked to help Marilyn pay for school."

"Didn't Aunt Marilyn get money from the government too?"

"Nope. It was harder for girls to get any money."

"That's not fair!" Patsy protested. As she spoke, she heard their apartment door open.

"No, it's not, but that's how it was. A lot of people thought girls didn't need to be educated to get jobs. They said girls didn't need any training to be cooks or housekeepers. But also, the government was trying to get people to leave reservations. Maybe they thought the girls would be less likely to leave. Or more likely to go back."

"Are you talking about relocation?" Dad asked, walking into the kitchen. "Lots of history lessons going on around here recently."

"Patsy was wondering about Marilyn and me both being nurses," Mom explained. "So, it's more of a family history lesson."

"But Dad," Patsy asked, "why did the government want people to leave reservations?"

"They said we could have better lives in the cities. My parents said they wanted us to move away, forget our language and traditions, and turn into white people. My dad said I should take the money, get my diploma, and then come home."

"So why did you stay in Denver?" Patsy asked.

"Well, for Marilyn at first. But then I found another reason." Dad kissed Mom's cheek. "I met a pretty brunette. But that's enough history. Look what was in the mailbox." He held up a fat letter.

"From Marilyn?" Mom asked, eyes wide.

Dad nodded.

"Read it!"

March 2, 1973
Dear Tiyóspaye,

I'm sure you have seen news reports about what is going on here. So first, don't worry. Mom, Hank, and I are all safe and sound. But things are wild here. You could say it started when Dick Wilson became the new tribal president. He keeps giving all the tribal jobs to his friends and family. And he wants the Lakota to give up our claims to our land for a government buyout. Of course, the Bureau of Indian

Affairs won't do anything about it. And if anyone tries to stand up to Wilson, he sends his goons after them. Two weeks ago, a guy came into the hospital with broken ribs and a black eye. He told the white doctor his horse bucked him off. But he told me some goons beat him up.

Well, back on February 22, some of the more traditional locals and a few people from AIM tried to impeach Wilson, but it didn't work. They kept meeting to figure out what they could do. It seems like they decided on this occupation on the spur of the moment. They didn't take any food or supplies with them. Or maybe they thought it would be over fast. But that very first night, the government surrounded Wounded Knee and blocked all the roads. Some of the people who live there have come out. They're staying with family and friends or at a Red Cross shelter in town.

At first, the news said AIM took hostages, but that's not true. The "hostages" were people living in Wounded Knee who don't support AIM but decided to stay anyway. Maybe they just didn't feel like sleeping on someone else's floor. But a lot of people do support AIM, and they're staying. That includes dozens of children and grandparents.

Snipers and a machine gun are posted on the roof of the BIA building in Pine Ridge. That's where the FBI set up their headquarters. They've got FBI agents, federal marshals, BIA cops, Department of Justice people, and Wilson's goons all running around with guns, and no one seems to know who is in charge. I'm afraid someone will get shot just because they don't know what they're doing. The first night, a teenager with AIM came into the hospital with half his hand blown off. He was probably using some old hunting rifle and didn't know how to load it right. Meanwhile, the schools are closed—so Hank seems to think this is a holiday! One of the government bunkers is less than two miles from our place. Close enough that we've heard some of the gunfire at night.

I hope this is all worth it in the end. In the meantime, if we have any trouble, I'll call from the hospital, but it will have to be a collect call. So, accept the charges, okay? We all miss you.

Thečhíȟila,
Marilyn (and Mom and Hank)

"I'm so relieved they're safe," Mom said. Dad nodded.

"Dad, what is that word at the beginning?" Patsy asked.

"Tiyóspaye," Dad said. "It means 'family.' Your parents and brothers and sisters, but also grandparents, cousins, aunts, uncles. And even more than that. Anyone who feels like kin can be adopted into your tiyóspaye."

Patsy nodded. "And who are the goons Aunt Marilyn talked about?"

"When Dick Wilson got elected, he started using the tribe's money to pay guys to scare anyone he didn't like. They've broken windows, slashed tires, and beaten people up. Even firebombed a few houses. Wilson called them 'security,' but most people called them goons. So, they named themselves Guardians of the Oglala Nation, or GOONs. They thought it was a pretty clever joke. But no one else was laughing."

"How long do you think this will go on?" Patsy asked.

Mom and Dad looked at each other.

"That's hard to say," Mom said. "A lot of people are scared and angry about problems that are difficult to fix."

Chapter 4

March 16, 1973

*P*atsy and Laura were seated at their usual table in the cafeteria when a boy's voice rang out from the table behind them. "I heard they are sending tanks. If AIM doesn't get out soon, they'll just run them out."

"Laura, I think he's talking about Wounded Knee," Patsy said, her voice low. She wasn't surprised. The occupation was into its third week. She heard kids at school talking about it almost every day.

Laura nodded. "Let's listen."

"I doubt it," came another voice—a girl's. "My mom said the protesters stayed on Alcatraz for over a year."

"But they couldn't get tanks into Alcatraz because it was an island," the boy replied. Patsy recognized the voice as Frank's. "Up at Wounded Knee, tanks could just roll right into that district. That would be so cool."

"Why do they call it Wounded Knee, anyway?" the girl asked. "Did someone hurt their knee there, like in a battle or something?"

"Maybe. There was a battle there," Frank said. "The army was fighting the Indians, and the army won. That's why the protesters chose Wounded Knee for the occupation. They're still sore about it."

Patsy's cheeks flushed with anger. "That's not what happened at all," she whispered to Laura. "The army shot hundreds of unarmed Lakota."

"So why don't you set him straight?" Laura asked.

Patsy shook her head. "He probably wouldn't believe me anyway. But I don't want to keep listening to this. Let's go sit somewhere else."

The girls took their trays to the other side of the cafeteria. From their new spot next to a window, Patsy watched a robin snatch up a bug. Then the bird flew into the boughs of a pine tree and disappeared.

"Do you want your cookie?" Laura asked.

Patsy eyed the half-eaten corn dog and cookie left on her tray. She wasn't hungry anymore. "Nah, you can have it."

As Laura munched, Patsy watched for the robin. Sometimes she wished she could hide like that bird.

~

All afternoon, Patsy couldn't stop thinking about what Frank had said at lunch. She wondered how many people knew the truth about what had happened at Wounded Knee—and how many believed rumors and lies. When the final bell rang, Patsy joined the rush for the door, but Miss Ashman called her back.

"This was excellent, Patricia," she said, handing Patsy back her report with a big red A penciled across the top. "Would you be interested in sharing it with the class?"

"Thanks," Patsy said. "But I don't think so."

"Suit yourself," Miss Ashman said. "But if you change your mind, please let me know. With what's been going on at Wounded Knee the past couple of weeks, it's important history for your classmates to know about."

Outside, Patsy scanned the parking lot for their old pickup truck. Mom wasn't working today, so she was picking Patsy up. She spotted the truck in the line of cars snaking around the school parking lot, but Dad was at the wheel. Mom was in the passenger seat. Patsy wondered what the special occasion was for Dad to leave work early.

Patsy skipped to the truck. She tossed her backpack in as she slid into the narrow back seat. "What are you doing here, Dad?"

"Nice to see you too," Dad said.

"I mean, what's going on? You shouldn't get off work for a couple hours."

"We have a surprise," Mom said, smiling widely.

"Last time you said that, I found out I was getting a little brother or sister."

"This isn't quite that good. But close. Just wait and see!"

Dad steered out of the parking lot, but when he got to the stop sign where they usually turned left, he went right. A few minutes later, he pulled into the driveway of a little brick house. A half-circle window divided into wedge-shaped panes decorated the front door. It reminded Patsy of a rising sun. A spreading ash tree shaded the front yard—or it would when it leafed out in a few weeks.

"Whose house is this?" Patsy asked.

"Ours!" Mom said. "At least it will be in a month or two if everything goes well."

"You found a house to buy?" Patsy was practically shouting with excitement.

Mom nodded. "With a bedroom for you and one for the new baby. And you won't have to change schools."

"Woo-hoo!" Patsy yelped. "Can we see the inside?"

"Yes. The real estate agent should be waiting to let us in. We wanted you to see it." Mom pulled a tape measure from her pocket. "And I need to measure for curtains."

Sure enough, a smiling middle-aged man opened the door before they could even knock. The house wasn't large, but it was bigger than their apartment. Whoever had lived there before had already moved out, leaving the house bare. It felt like it was waiting for a new family.

The living room opened into a dining room, which led into the kitchen. Down the hall, Patsy found four doors. She tried them all. First came a small bedroom that looked out onto the front yard. Next was a big bedroom with two closets. That would be her parents', she guessed. Then was the bathroom, with gleaming tile the color of a robin's egg. Last was a cozy bedroom with buttery-yellow walls and a view of the backyard. A stand of pine trees filled one corner and a swing set sat opposite. Patsy was getting too old for swing sets, but she could imagine pushing a little sister on one.

Coming up from behind, Dad gave Patsy's shoulder a little squeeze.

"We thought this room would be yours," he said. "We can paint the walls if you don't like the color."

"No," Patsy said. "It's just right the way it is."

A few minutes later, with the window measurements completed, the family piled back into the truck.

"So, we'll move in a month or two?" Patsy asked.

"That's the plan, if everything goes through."

Something about Mom's tone made Patsy worry. "What could go wrong?" she asked.

Mom sighed, but Dad smiled.

"A lot has already gone right," Dad said. "We have the money saved for the down payment. We made an offer, and it was accepted. All that's left is to get a loan from the bank for the mortgage."

"Are you worried the bank will turn you down?"

"They shouldn't," Dad said. "Mom and I both have steady jobs."

"But sometimes bankers find reasons to turn people down if they know they aren't white," said Mom.

For the second time in one day, Patsy's cheeks warmed with anger. "That should be illegal!"

"It *is* illegal," Mom said. "Although it's only been illegal for about five years. But it can be hard to prove that racism was the reason someone turned down your loan. A lot of bankers are honest, but you just never know who you're dealing with. So, we're playing it safe. I went into the bank to fill out the application without Dad. I just had to bring it home for him to sign. I took it back today. They should never know Dad is Lakota."

Patsy's excitement wilted as she thought about Dad having to hide who he was. Would Patsy have to do that too someday? Hide who she was to get a house? Or a job? So far, she hadn't told anyone at school except Laura that she was Lakota. Was she hiding who she was already?

Chapter 5

March 27, 1973

$\mathcal{P}$atsy was watching the evening news with Dad again. It had been a month since the occupation started, and for the first couple of weeks, there had been news about it every day. The TV news had included footage of men huddling inside their bunkers, carrying guns, talking on walkie-talkies, and taking cover behind armored cars. Pictures in the newspapers had showed a white church on a little hill next to the grave site from the 1890 massacre. The occupiers were using it for gatherings during the day and a place to sleep at night. A tipi near the church was used for smaller meetings.

But for the last several days, reports had been scant and confusing. One day they said negotiations were going badly. The next day they claimed an agreement might come soon. Some people said Communists were backing the occupiers, giving them money and guns. AIM said that wasn't true. Two days ago, a marshal was shot and paralyzed. AIM blamed Dick Wilson's goons. The US government blamed AIM. And yesterday, Wilson set up a new roadblock, and no one knew if the FBI had approved it.

Patsy didn't know what to believe. Sometimes she thought she should try to ignore the whole thing. What could she do about it anyway? But every night, she found herself next to Dad when the news started, hoping for more information. Tonight, they watched the whole broadcast, but there was nothing about Wounded Knee.

"Maybe reporters are starting to lose interest," Dad said.

"The Vietnam War has been going on as long as I can remember," Patsy said, "and they're still reporting on that."

"People care so much about the war because so many soldiers have died in Vietnam. If they are losing interest in Wounded Knee because no one is dying, that's a good thing. But I hope it won't take a martyr to get people's attention again."

Patsy heard familiar footsteps coming up their apartment steps. Mom was home from work.

"Did you save me any dinner?" Mom asked, opening the front door.

"There's meat loaf in the oven keeping warm," Dad said.

"I can get it!" Patsy hopped up and went to the kitchen to grab a plate.

As Mom got more pregnant, she seemed more tired. Especially after a day of work. Mom and Dad joined Patsy as she set a dish of meat loaf and green beans on the table.

"Heard some gossip at the hospital today," Mom said around a mouthful of dinner. "One of the nurses has a cousin who works for NBC. She said that he says that almost all the press have been booted out of Wounded Knee. NBC was the last television network with people there, and they were ordered out yesterday. They're only allowed to go to the government press conferences in Pine Ridge. And the FBI has cut the phone lines into Wounded Knee. So no one can even be interviewed by phone. The government says it's an order from the tribal court. But NBC thinks the FBI put them up to it."

"So that's why there was nothing on the news tonight," Patsy said.

"If the rumor is true, yes," Mom agreed. "But that's not all. NBC is also broadcasting the Oscars tonight. And some of the people at NBC are saying that if Marlon Brando wins the award for best actor, he's going to refuse it."

"Why would he refuse it?" Patsy wondered.

"That's the best part. He wants to show support for the protesters at Wounded Knee!"

Patsy didn't think she had ever seen a Marlon Brando movie, but she had seen his pictures on TV and in the magazines at the grocery store.

"Is Marlon Brando Native?" she asked. He didn't look Native.

Dad chuckled. "No, he's white. But you don't have to be Indian to look at what's happening and think it's not right."

"Can we watch the Oscars, please?" Patsy asked. "I want to see if he wins. And if he really will refuse."

"It's a school night," Mom said, "and the awards ceremony lasts for hours. They always do best actor at the end. It might be pretty late."

"I promise I'll go straight to bed," said Patsy. "I'll get all ready for bed before it starts."

"Do you have homework?"

"It's done," Patsy said.

"It's just one night," Dad said. "She might witness history."

"Fine." Mom sighed. "I'm way too tired to argue with both of you. But it starts soon, so hurry up."

The awards show was already underway when Patsy, pajamas on and teeth brushed, curled up beside Dad on the couch. Mom was right about it being long. Patsy waited through awards for editing, music, costumes, and all kinds of things. Mom had fallen asleep on Dad's other shoulder by the time they finally announced the presenters for best actor. Patsy woke her up as a familiar-looking man (maybe someone Patsy had seen on TV?) and a woman in an expensive-looking dress read the names of all the actors in the running.

"The winner is . . ." The woman paused to open the envelope. "Marlon Brando!"

The usual applause began in the auditorium. The camera cut to follow Marlon Brando coming up from the audience.

Except it wasn't Marlon Brando. It was a woman—a woman in a traditional Native dress with hair the same color as Patsy's. Her hair was gathered into long ponytails held by beaded and fringed bands on either side of her face. She was beautiful. Her fringed buckskin dress was decorated with colorful beads and looked just as elegant as any Patsy had seen that night.

The presenters offered her the little golden Oscar statue. She held up one hand to refuse. Then she took her place behind the microphone.

"Hello, my name is Sacheen Littlefeather," she announced. "I'm Apache, and I am president of the National Native American Affirmative Image Committee. I'm representing Marlon Brando this evening, and he has asked me to tell you that he very regretfully cannot accept this very generous award. And the reasons for this being the treatment of American Indians today by the film industry—"

Loud booing broke out.

Littlefeather looked down at the podium. "Excuse me."

Someone started clapping, and soon applause drowned out the boos.

Littlefeather looked at the crowd and continued.

"—and on television and movie reruns. And also with recent happenings at Wounded Knee. I beg that in the future, our hearts and our understandings will meet with love and generosity."

She left the stage with applause filling the auditorium. Patsy was proud of her. She had been so calm and graceful even when people tried to silence her.

"Wow," Mom said. "I didn't expect that. That was worth staying up for."

Dad nodded, smiling.

"What did she mean, 'the treatment of American Indians by the film industry'?" Patsy asked.

"Think about the times you have seen Indians in movies or television," Dad said. "What were they doing? What did they say?"

Patsy chewed her thumbnail. "Well, mostly they were attacking cowboys. Or the cowboys were shooting at them. And as far as I can remember, they didn't say much of anything. Even Tonto. He hardly talks, except to agree with the Lone Ranger."

"That's exactly what she means, Pats. Native Americans are shown as savages if they're shown at all. Mostly they're the bad guys so you can root for the cowboys to win. When they get any lines, the Indians sound ignorant. And until more Native people get jobs making movies and TV shows, that probably won't change."

Patsy looked back at the TV. There were millions of people watching Sacheen Littlefeather tonight. Maybe that would help. She wasn't savage or ignorant. She was elegant and smart.

"Do you think this will help the people at Wounded Knee?" Patsy asked.

"Can't hurt," Dad said.

Mom, yawning, crossed the living room to turn the TV off.

"Time for bed," she said. "For all of us."

Chapter 6

April 3–6, 1973

A week later, Patsy was concentrating so intently on her math homework that she jumped when the phone rang. She ran to the living room to answer it.

"Hello, Antoine residence," Patsy answered with her best phone manners.

"I have a collect call for Daniel or Judy Antoine from South Dakota," said an unfamiliar voice. "Will you accept the charges?"

Patsy's stomach dropped. Aunt Marilyn said she'd call if there was trouble. Was this bad news?

"Yes, we'll accept the charges." Patsy nervously twisted the phone cord's spirals around her finger. She heard a click as the operator left the call. "Aunt Marilyn, is that you?"

"Yes, Patsy. It's your auntie."

"Are you okay?"

"Yes, honey," Aunt Marilyn said. "We're all fine. Perfectly safe."

Patsy exhaled. She hadn't realized she'd been holding her breath.

"But I have a problem I hope your dad will help with," Aunt Marilyn continued. "Is he home?"

"No, he's still at work."

"Can you give him a message? I'm calling from the hospital, and I don't want to stick him with the bill for another long-distance call."

"Sure. Should I write it down?"

"No, that's okay. Tell him the pump is broken on our well. It went out yesterday, so we don't have any running water. He's the one who installed it in the first place. I'm hoping he can come up here and fix it."

"Okay. I can tell him. But how can he get in touch with you?"

"Have him call the hospital. He has the number. The receptionist will find me. I talked to her about it. I work until seven today and tomorrow."

"Got it," Patsy said. "Are you sure you're okay? The news on TV hasn't been good."

"That's true," Aunt Marilyn agreed. "The government sent a new guy to be the head honcho last week. He's really cracking down. He stopped letting food and medical supplies through the roadblocks and just cut off water and electricity to Wounded Knee. Of course, a lot of the locals never have water or power, so I think they'll figure out ways to get by. But we're safe. We've kept our distance from the bunkers and roadblocks, and so far, no one has bothered us."

"That's a relief."

"Also, there is talk of another cease-fire. I think the government is getting tired of the bad press. They already have enough of that to deal with from Watergate. Or maybe the occupiers are getting tired of being cold and hungry. Either way, I hope it will be over sooner rather than later."

"I hope so too," said Patsy.

"Listen, honey, I better quit yakking, or this call is going to cost your folks an arm and a leg. Thanks for being my messenger. Bye."

Patsy hung up the receiver. She tried to go back to her math homework but couldn't concentrate. She kept watching the clock, calculating the minutes until Dad would be home instead of calculating the answers to her problems. She was anxious to tell him the news, but she also had an idea. A thought had sprouted almost as soon as she'd hung up the phone. Patsy wanted to go to Pine Ridge with her dad. Worrying about her family had made her anxious to see them again. Plus, she had recently watched history unfold on TV. Now she had a chance to see it happening in real life.

When Dad finally came through the door, Patsy spilled all the news from her aunt.

But Dad just said, "Hmm."

"Well, are you going to South Dakota?" Patsy asked.

"Let's talk about it when Mom gets home."

Patsy waited through dinner and dishes and the rest of her homework. She waited as the clock ticked past the time her mom usual got home. But finally, Mom arrived, thirteen minutes later than usual.

"Aunt Marilyn called, and everyone is fine, but their pump is broken, so they don't have any running water. She wants Dad to come and fix it, as soon as he can. And she thinks there will be a cease-fire soon. Then the whole occupation might be over. So will Dad go to South Dakota?" Patsy related all the news without stopping for a single breath.

"Slow down, Patsy," Mom said. "What is all this about a pump and South Dakota?"

Patsy drew a long breath to start again, but Dad held up his hand.

"Marilyn called to say the pump went out on the well," Dad said. "She's hoping I can come up there and fix it."

Mom looked at him. "Do you think you can? You don't even know what's wrong with it."

"Some people say I can fix anything," Dad teased, reminding Mom of her own words. "I'll take some parts and tools with me. I'll fix it, one way or another. With the occupation still going on, it might be hard to find someone else to do it. And it could get expensive. Besides, there are always other jobs that need doing around the place. It's been too long since I was back there to help out."

"When do you want to go?" asked Mom.

"I was thinking I'd leave work a little early on Friday. Get there in time to get a decent night's sleep. Then I've got the weekend to work. If I can finish up by Monday or Tuesday, I'll miss only a couple days of work."

Mom nodded. Patsy took advantage of the silence to bring up her idea.

"I want to go too," she said. "I have spring break next week, so I wouldn't miss any school. And I haven't been to South Dakota since Grandfather's funeral."

Mom stopped nodding. "No, Patsy. It's too dangerous. You've seen the news. Everybody's running around with guns, and they're shooting at each other practically every night."

"But Aunt Marilyn said there will be a cease-fire very soon." Patsy knew that might be stretching the truth, but she just *had* to go to Pine Ridge. "And I'll be with Dad. Hank is almost two years younger than me, and *he's* fine."

"Maybe we can all go this summer, after the baby comes and this occupation ends," Mom offered. "It would be more fun in the summer anyway. South Dakota is still plenty cold in April."

"Why don't we all go now?" Patsy suggested. "Then you can keep an eye on me too."

"Mom is saving her time off for when the baby comes," Dad said. "And I don't think she wants to sleep on a cot and use an outhouse when she's six months pregnant."

Mom smiled gratefully.

"But Judy," Dad said, "maybe Patsy should come. It will only be a few days. And the house is more than two miles from Wounded Knee. We'll keep a safe distance."

Now Patsy smiled gratefully. "Please, Mom. It's important."

"Why is it so important to go now? Why can't it wait?"

"It's something Laura said."

"And exactly what did Laura say?" Mom demanded.

"She said that for a girl who is half Lakota, I don't know much about being Lakota."

"Pats, there is more than one way to be Lakota," Dad said. "You know that, right?"

"Yeah, I just feel like I need to figure out *my* way to be Lakota. And seeing our family might help."

Mom sighed. "Okay," she said, hands on her hips. "But you have to promise to be smart and stay safe."

~

Over the next couple of days, Dad gathered tools and supplies, things he thought he might need to fix the pump. A couple gallons of paint went into the back of the truck as well. If the weather was warm enough, he would paint the wood siding that covered half the house. He also packed an old camping cot for Patsy; he would take the couch. He called the hospital and told Aunt Marilyn they would arrive Friday night.

Mom fretted but helped Patsy pack warm clothes. She was relieved when, on Thursday, the news reported a cease-fire had been reached. She also called the school to excuse Patsy early on Friday.

Paying attention was always hard on the last day before a break, but Friday seemed to drag on and on. During lunch and recess, all the kids talked about spring break plans. A couple of kids were going skiing. One boy was even going to Disneyland. But most kids in the school were staying home or, like Patsy, visiting relatives. Their families didn't have the money for trips to California.

Laura, who wasn't going anywhere, was jealous. "I'm going to be so bored. I hope we at least get some warm weather so I won't be stuck inside all week."

"I'll probably be back Tuesday or Wednesday," Patsy reassured her friend. "We can bike to the library or the Dairy Queen. Or both."

"At least send me a postcard," Laura said. "Getting some mail might be the highlight of my whole week."

"I promise," Patsy said.

When they returned to the classroom after lunch, Patsy found a small book sitting on her desk. Curious, she opened the cover and found neatly lined pages. A spot for a date topped each one. A little note was slipped inside.

Dear Patricia,

Your mother explained that you will be leaving today to visit your relatives on the Pine Ridge Indian Reservation. I was surprised to hear that you have family there. You haven't mentioned that in class. Considering the historic events transpiring on Pine Ridge, I thought perhaps you would want to record some of your thoughts. Though your experiences need not be historic to be worth remembering—with the passage of time, even mundane things sometimes prove remarkable.

Sincerely,
Miss Ashman

Patsy was surprised. Miss Ashman was always so formal and strict. But sending this journal was really thoughtful. Maybe, when she wasn't standing in front of a classroom, Miss Ashman was pretty nice.

Patsy tucked the little book into her backpack. Checking the clock, she realized that in about eight hours, she would be getting ready for bed in South Dakota.

Chapter 7

April 7, 1973

April 7, 1973

I'm in South Dakota! The drive was long, but the first half was pretty fun. Almost as soon as we got outside of Denver, the scenery changed. Wide open land was dotted with pine trees and scrubby bushes. The rocky ravines and hills are nothing like the mountains, but still beautiful. We saw antelope and pronghorns and, near dusk, a coyote. After the sun went down, though, there wasn't much to look at. Mom packed us ham and cheese sandwiches. She even remembered to leave the mayo off mine. We ate in the car and only stopped for gas.

We got into the town of Pine Ridge after dark. It's tiny compared to Denver. A couple inches of fresh snow covered the town and made the night brighter. Dad pointed out the BIA office. The sandbags piled on the roof almost looked like snow drifts. But there was no mistaking the machine gun. Dad also showed me his old school and the hospital where Aunt Marilyn works.

To get to the house, we went east another eight miles or so. Then we turned north and bumped along a dirt road for about five miles. Dad said Wounded Knee is just a couple of miles farther north and east from here. The closest government bunker is in same direction as Wounded Knee, but half a mile closer. There's also a roadblock about a mile and a half east of us. So, I'm not allowed off family property.

In the moonlight, the house reminded me of a turtle, small and low but sturdy looking. The oldest part is the one-room log cabin. It's the kitchen and living room now. That's where Dad and I are sleeping. On the south side is a smaller room that was added on. Grandma and Aunt Marilyn use that for their bedroom. Hank is sharing with them while we're visiting. On the north side is a little lean-to that Dad and Grandfather added to be the bathroom about ten years ago. It's like the head of the turtle sticking out of its shell. The little window in the door even looks like the turtle's eye.

Dad explained the plumbing and power system he built for the house. They have a gas-powered generator that powers the pump for the well and one outlet inside the house. They turn it on long enough for the pump to fill a water tank behind the house. Then water from the tank runs to the kitchen sink and the bathroom when you turn on a faucet. They drain to a little gully behind the house. In the summer, the water feeds Grandma's garden. Since the pump broke, they've been using the old hand pump to fill buckets. Sometimes they use the outlet to power a radio, but there's no TV. The house is heated by a woodstove. I think Dad was *so smart to figure all that out. There's no sewer though, so everyone still uses the outhouse. That was a cold walk first thing this morning!*

Grandma had hot fry bread and honey waiting for us last night. It was delicious. I hope she'll teach me how to make it. Aunt Marilyn is making scrambled eggs on the woodstove for everyone for breakfast. The eggs are from Grandma's chickens. A lot of things are different from home. But that makes it feel like more of an adventure!

The talk over breakfast was about the occupation. Patsy sprinkled salt on her eggs and listened.

"Anyone we know out at Wounded Knee?" Dad asked.

"Oh, yes," Grandma said. "You remember the Lamonts? I think you went to school with one of the girls."

"Sure," said Dad as he added some pepper to his eggs. "There are eight Lamont sisters. I think almost everyone went to school with one of the girls."

74

"Well, the only son—Buddy—he's out there with one of the girls, and a few nieces and nephews too. Some of the other grandkids are staying with Agnes."

"I thought he was in the Marines," Dad said around a mouthful of eggs.

"Just got home a few months ago," Aunt Marilyn said. "He had a job with the BIA cops, but then Dick Wilson got him fired."

"Why?" Dad asked.

"Maybe because he wouldn't go around harassing people like Wilson wanted him to. Or maybe because his mom isn't afraid to say what she thinks of Wilson."

"Agnes?" Dad asked. "Has Agnes turned into an activist?"

"You'd be surprised what some of us old ladies can do when we put our minds to it," Grandma said. "Many of the older, traditional women were among the Lakota who asked AIM to come in the first place. Some, like Agnes, have been protesting at the BIA. Several others are inside Wounded Knee as part of the occupation. A couple of old medicine men too."

"Who would have thought," Dad said.

"But everyone may be coming out soon," Aunt Marilyn said cheerfully. "While you two were on your way here, Russell Means was traveling to Washington, DC. He is supposed to meet with White House officials this weekend. AIM wants them to agree to investigate Wilson and set up talks about restoring treaty rights. If they agree, the occupiers will leave."

Hank, who had been silently shoveling in his breakfast as fast as he could, swallowed his last bite.

"Hey, Patsy, want to see my new BB gun?" He sounded like a little kid anxious to show off a new toy. "We can shoot targets."

Patsy looked at her dad.

"Go ahead," he said. "But don't shoot your eye out. Your mother will have my hide if I bring you home injured. And stay close to the house. We might need to go into town after I look at that pump."

A few minutes later, cocooned in her coat and scarf, Patsy helped Hank set up a row of old cans on some overturned milk crates.

Hank took twenty paces back and scratched a line in the dirt with a stick.

"I'll show you how to do it first," he said, sounding more like a schoolteacher than a ten-year-old.

Hank pointed out where he had loaded the BBs. Then he gave the lever below the trigger a couple pumps.

"That's the sight," he said, pointing to a little metal tab at the end of the barrel. "Line that up with your target. And . . ."

Hank pulled the trigger. The popping sound from the gun was immediately followed by a metallic clink. A can fell to the ground.

"Nice shot," Patsy said.

"Yeah, I'm pretty good."

"Can I try now?"

"I think you should watch a couple more," Hank said.

Patsy rolled her eyes. That was just like a boy. It wasn't rocket science. You just pointed and pulled the trigger. A couple more shots turned into a dozen. Five more cans hit the ground before Hank handed over the gun.

Patsy lined the sight up with one of the remaining cans. She fired. There was a pop, but no clink. She tried again. And again. And again. Finally, a can hit the dirt.

"Not bad," Hank said, "for a beginner."

After a few more shots, they reset the cans. Behind the firing line again, Hank took the gun back.

"Mom says I can use the real rifle in a few years. Then I can start hunting. I bet I get my first deer before I'm thirteen." Hank took aim and shot. A can tipped over.

Patsy wasn't sure what to say. She didn't think she'd like hunting. But Hank went right on talking.

"I wish this occupation would have happened when I was older so I could have gone to help. Mom won't let me anywhere near Wounded Knee. It's only a couple miles that way, you know." Hank pointed off to the northeast. "I could hike there, but if I even look in that direction, Mom or Grandma makes me come inside."

Patsy had wanted to come to South Dakota so badly, and she hoped she might get a look at Wounded Knee. But she wasn't like Hank—she didn't want to pick up a gun and go join the protesters. That sounded dangerous and scary.

And she wasn't sure that all the shooting was accomplishing anything. She thought about the teenager who had blown up his hand the first night of the occupation. He had been a kid like Hank just a few years ago.

"They just want you to be safe," Patsy told her cousin.

"Shh," Hank hissed, suddenly pointing off to the left of the targets.

"What?" Patsy whispered.

"Jackrabbit."

Patsy scanned the landscape of mottled gray and brown and white, but she didn't see anything.

Pop! Hank fired. Patsy jumped. Was he trying to kill the rabbit?

"I think I got it!" he yelped, and ran off.

Following behind him, Patsy saw the rabbit lying on its side, its hind legs twitching. "You hurt it!"

"Well, I hit it," Hank said defensively.

"What do we do now?" Patsy asked. Hank stood frozen for a few seconds. Then he pointed the BB gun at the rabbit.

"Stop!" It was Dad's voice. He was walking toward them, a rifle in his right hand. He didn't look happy. He stopped about fifty feet away. "Come here."

When Patsy and Hank were safely behind him, Dad aimed and fired. The rabbit quit moving.

Then Dad looked hard at Hank. "You don't shoot animals for fun. When you're older, you can hunt. But only for what you need. Understand?"

Hank swallowed and nodded.

"You shot it, so it's your job to skin it for dinner. You know how?" Dad asked.

Hank nodded again, but hesitantly, like maybe he didn't really know how.

"If you run into trouble, ask Grandma for help," Dad said. "She can skin a jackrabbit almost quicker than you can shoot it. Well, go get it."

Hank trotted off to collect the rabbit.

"Dad, you're a good shot," Patsy said. "I've never even seen you with a gun before."

"I don't have a gun in Denver. There's nothing I need to shoot."

Chapter 8

April 7, 1973

*T*hrough the glass of the truck's windows, the sun finally felt warm as Patsy and her dad pulled into the town of Pine Ridge. They were looking for some supplies to fix the pump. Hank had looked like he might cry when Dad told him he had to stay home and finish cleaning the rabbit. Patsy felt a little sorry for him, but he was the one who'd shot the rabbit.

"So, what's wrong with the pump?" Patsy asked.

"Turned out to be simple," Dad said. "The wires going from the generator to the pump are inside a metal tube to protect them. Every time the pump turned on, they rubbed a little against the metal. After years of that, some of the insulation rubbed clean off."

"You can fix it," Patsy said. "I knew you could."

Dad smiled. "If I can get a long enough length of wire. I brought some with me, but not enough. We'll try the service station."

A minute later, they parked in front of a gas station. A bell on the door jingled as they went in. Patsy noticed a little rack of postcards next to the cash register. She remembered her promise to Laura.

At the sound of the bell, a man about her dad's age looked up from his stool behind the counter. A wide grin spread across his face.

"Is that Danny Antoine?" the man asked.

"Pete?" Dad said.

"That's right, man," the guy—Pete—said. "I haven't seen you since your dad's funeral."

"It has been a while," Dad said. "Your hair is longer. How long you been working here?"

"A couple years. It beats working on the road crew in the dead of winter."

"I bet," Dad chuckled. "Oh, hey, this is my daughter, Patsy."

"Nice to meet you, Patsy. Your dad and I went to high school together."

"Nice to meet you too," Patsy said.

"What brings you back home?" Pete asked. "You aren't here to join the occupation, are you? I've had all kinds of people in here trying to get to Wounded Knee. Cops, reporters, hippies, preachers. Even a few college kids who thought they'd spend spring break playing warrior."

"Nah, that's not it," Dad said. "The pump's broken at my family's place. I came up to fix it. Actually, I was hoping you might be able to help me out. I need about seventy feet of wire, 14-gauge or bigger. You got anything like that?"

"Let me check around in back." Pete disappeared behind a door.

While they waited, Patsy browsed the postcards.

"Dad, it doesn't look like any of these postcards are from Pine Ridge," she said.

"It's not exactly a tourist spot, Pats. There isn't even a hotel for forty miles."

Patsy chose a card featuring the Black Hills at sunset. She knew the Black Hills were sacred to the Lakota. When she was researching her report, she had read about how Custer and some white miners had invaded them looking for gold.

Pete returned, empty-handed. "Sorry, Dan. I got some shorter pieces but nothing close to seventy feet."

"Well, thanks for checking," Dad said. "Maybe I'll try the hardware store in Hot Springs. Just thought I'd save the drive if I could."

Pete's face got serious. "I'd avoid Hot Springs right now. Same for all the other white border towns. You know that's how all this started, right? Wesley Bad Heart Bull got killed by some white thugs in Buffalo Gap."

"I heard something about that," said Dad.

"It looked like they might get away without any jail time. Wilson and his mixed-blood friends weren't going to do anything about it. So, some of the full-bloods got AIM to come. They went to the courthouse in Custer to demand justice."

"Which turned into a riot, the way I heard it," Dad said. "AIM torched some cars. Burned down a building and a couple of gas stations."

"Yeah, but only after the cops wouldn't even let them into the courthouse. Even made the victim's poor old mother stand out in a snowstorm. Then they arrested her after."

Patsy hadn't heard anything about this. Whatever Dad knew, he hadn't shared with her.

"Anyway, things are pretty tense in the white towns," Pete said. "Plenty of rednecks who are just itching to pick a fight with an Indian. I'd steer clear, especially with a kid along."

"Any idea where I could get that wire on the reservation?" Dad asked.

"Let me ask around," Pete said. "Give me a couple days. I bet I can find some."

"All right," Dad agreed, with a quick look at Patsy. "Thanks, Pete. In the meantime, I need this postcard. And a pack of Wrigley's."

Patsy raised her eyebrows as Dad put the chewing gum on the counter. He wasn't a gum chewer.

"For Hank," Dad explained.

Back in the truck, Patsy chewed her thumbnail. "Dad, when Pete was talking about mixed-bloods, he was talking about people like me, right? People who have a Native parent and grandparents and a white parent and grandparents?"

Dad sighed. "There are some people who think Native people should only marry other Native people and have Native children. They might call someone a mixed-blood if that person has white ancestors. There are also people who don't care how light or dark your skin is but think Indians should keep all their traditional ways. They don't like anything that comes from whites. And they might call someone mixed-blood if the way that person talks or thinks seems too white."

"But you don't agree with them?" Patsy asked. "You moved to Denver and married a white woman."

"I married the woman I fell in love with, who happens to be white. And when we thought about where to raise a family, we knew it could be tough for us, and for you, anywhere we went. But we both had jobs in Denver, so we stayed. I hope we made the right choice."

"Do you support AIM?" Patsy asked.

"I support almost everything they say. The white men who have been running the government for the last two hundred years have broken every treaty and promise they ever made to us and all the Native nations. They pushed us off our land and forced us onto reservations. When killing us outright didn't work, they tried to erase us by making us forget our languages, religions, and cultures. And now Dick Wilson is trying to set himself up as a dictator, but the US government won't do anything about it. They say it's our problem. But they've always been eager to interfere in our lives when they have something to gain. So I understand why people are so angry. And we do need to stand up for our rights and keep our traditions. Still, I don't support everything AIM does. Burning down a building won't restore our treaty rights or bring back the buffalo or teach anyone to speak Lakota. I'm not sure taking over a district will either."

As they drove along the main street in town, they passed a little café, an empty lot, a laundromat, and an abandoned building. The buildings all needed new coats of paint. The lots needed weeding.

"So, what would help?" Patsy asked.

Dad shook his head. "I wish I knew."

～

Before heading back, they stopped at the little grocery store. Dad wanted to leave the family's pantry well stocked. They pushed their cart into the checkout line.

"I forgot the coffee," Dad said. "Can you hold our spot, Pats? I'll be right back."

Patsy waited as the older woman in front of her began unloading a cart brimming with staples like flour, rice, and beans.

"What's all this for, Mrs. Lamont?" the clerk asked. Patsy remembered that name—Lamont. Was this Agnes Lamont, the woman her grandmother had talked about?

"Just stocking up," Mrs. Lamont said.

"This is a lot more than you usually buy," the clerk said suspiciously. Patsy noticed that he was white.

"Like I said. Stocking up on a few things."

The clerk stopped ringing up her items. "I heard you've got kids out at Wounded Knee. You wouldn't be trying to smuggle food out there, would you? You got fifty pounds of rice here. What are you going to do with that much rice?"

Patsy bristled. There was no law against buying rice. No matter who it was for. Patsy's anger made her forget she was shy.

"Hello, Mrs. Lamont," she called, waving cheerfully.

Mrs. Lamont turned. Her questioning look showed she wondered why this strange girl was striking up a conversation in the grocery store.

"You probably don't remember me." Patsy doubted she'd ever met Agnes Lamont, but she pressed ahead anyway. "I'm Dan Antoine's daughter. We're here visiting my grandma and Aunt Marilyn."

"Always nice to have young people home to visit. Tell your grandma I said hey," Mrs. Lamont said. "Haven't seen her in a spell."

"I'll do that," Patsy said. "I heard you got some of your grandkids staying with you. Lots of extra mouths to feed, I bet."

Mrs. Lamont winked at her, then looked at the clerk. "That's right, I have a houseful right now. And I got a couple dozen more grandkids besides them. Never know who will be showing up for dinner. Makes it hard to keep the cupboards full."

The clerk eyed Patsy. Patsy smiled sweetly.

"I suppose," the clerk said, ringing up the next bag of rice.

Dad rejoined Patsy in line.

"Hey, Dan," Mrs. Lamont said.

Dad looked surprised. "That you, Mrs. Lamont? Nice to see you."

She nodded. "That's a nice girl you got. Smart too."

"Um, thank you," Dad said. Mrs. Lamont put the last brown bag in her cart and headed toward the door.

"What's that about?" he whispered to Patsy.

"I'll tell you later."

Chapter 9

April 9, 1973

April 9, 1973

The last two days have been busy. The weather warmed up enough to paint. Dad has Hank helping him with the scraping and sanding. I'm not sure how helpful Hank actually is, but he sure seems to like hanging out with Dad. When they're done painting, Dad says they'll fix the roof on the chicken coop. Aunt Marilyn had shifts at the hospital the last couple of days, so I have been helping Grandma. We fried the jackrabbit together. Hank seemed proud that he shot it. But he wasn't going to say that to Dad. It tasted like chicken.

Yesterday, we had a chicken from Grandma's flock. Guess who plucked it? Me! After Grandma wrung its neck, we dropped it in hot water and stirred it around for a minute. Then I pulled all the feathers off. It was kind of smelly.

Grandma and I also split a bunch of wood for the stove. I think Grandma can swing an ax as good as Dad. My aim wasn't as good. I swung the ax into the ground a couple of times. Grandma just said, "It's okay to hit the ground. Just don't hit your leg." She also taught me how to make fry bread. She told me how Native women invented fry bread after being forced onto reservations. When the buffalo were mostly gone, the government gave the tribes flour and salt and lard, all foods they weren't used to and didn't like. But the Native women figured out how to make something delicious from it—fry bread.

I'm excited for today. Grandma is teaching me to bead. She has a beautiful cradleboard that her mother and aunts made for her before Dad was born. Some of the beading needs to be fixed. And we

Patsy heard sawing outside. Dad and Hank must have started on the chicken coop. Grandma was unwrapping the cradleboard from the blanket that protected it. Was Dad really once small enough to be swaddled up in the layers of cloth and leather? Patsy imagined chubby baby cheeks and dark hair peeping out.

"Those boards remind me of little skis." Patsy pointed to the two flat pieces of wood sticking above the pouch that formed the back of the board.

"They are important," Grandma said. "They support the baby's back so it grows strong and straight. Often, Lakota women used to use buffalo hides for the pouch that swaddles the baby. But by the time your dad came along, if a baby got a cradleboard at all, it would usually be buckskin."

Thousands of yellow, red, black, white, and blue beads formed intricate designs on the buckskin. Patsy could only guess how many hours the women of her family had spent creating them. Grandma carefully threaded a needle.

"See these rows?" Grandma pointed to a diamond of red beads. "These are loose. We need to sew them all back down."

Grandma passed the needle through a half dozen beads, then back through the buckskin. "This is called lazy stitch. Now I'll go the other way through the next row."

As she worked, she talked.

"Did you know your dad was born right here, in this house? The hospital wasn't built yet. But even if it had been, I would have had him at home. Marilyn was born the year after the hospital opened, and she was born at home too. As long as my mother could come, I felt that I would be safe, and all would be well for the babies."

"I didn't know that," Patsy said.

"Of course, I didn't want to take any chances, so I also made a keya charm. *Keya* is Lakota for 'turtle.' It has a little pouch inside the shell. When your dad's navel cord fell off,

I put it inside the turtle pouch. We kept it safely hidden in the cradleboard. To protect the baby."

Patsy had never heard this story. "Why a turtle, Grandma?"

"Turtles may be slow and look rough, but they are tough. They live long and are hard to kill. Turtles are survivors. Here." She handed Patsy the needle. "You give it a try."

Patsy secured the next row. She held it up for Grandma to see.

"Very good. You're a natural." Grandma took the cradleboard back.

"What happened to the turtle charm—the keya? Do you still have it?"

"Oh yes. It would be bad luck to lose it." Grandma crossed the kitchen, pulled an old cracker tin from a drawer, and brought it back to Patsy. It was full of thread, strings of beads, and scraps of soft deer hide. Nestled in the middle was a little beaded turtle. Patsy scooped it into the palm of her hand and gently ran a finger over the shiny beads.

"It's beautiful," she said. Patsy thought of her mother and the new baby. The baby would be half Lakota, just like Patsy. What could Patsy tell the baby about being Lakota? "Grandma, can you teach me some more Lakota words?"

"Of course. What do you want to know?"

Patsy looked at the kaleidoscope of colors in the tin. "How do you say yellow?"

"Yellow is zí."

"Zí," Patsy repeated.

"Good. Zí is important. It is the color of the east, the rising sun, and new beginnings."

"How about red?"

"Šá. That is the color of the south, where the sun shines and makes things grow."

"Šá," Patsy said. "Šá and zí. Are there colors for the other directions?"

"Yes, sápa is black. It is for the west, where the sun sets and darkness comes. And ská is white, for the north. It is the color of the moon at night and the snow that flies on the winter winds."

"Sápa and ská," Patsy said. "Black and white. What about blue?"

"Blue is for the sky that is above all. Blue is tȟó," Grandma explained.

Patsy pointed to a string of yellow beads in the tin. "Zí," she said.

"Very good. And what is this?" Grandma held up a string of red beads.

"Šá. And those are sápa, ská, and tȟó," Patsy said, pointing to beads of black, white, and finally, blue.

"What a smart granddaughter I have!" Grandma was so pleased her face seemed to glow. "When you go home to Denver, keep practicing. Your father can teach you anything you want to say in Lakota. He hasn't forgotten."

Patsy nodded.

"Now, let's have some fun. You must choose a design for your hairbands," Grandma said.

Patsy replaced the keya while Grandma pulled strings of beads from the tin. They tried several ideas. Patsy's favorite was a design that looked like a yellow sunburst shining inside rings of white and blue. She measured and cut the buckskin. Then she calculated how many beads should be in each section of the design. She hadn't expected to use fractions for making hairbands, but they came in handy. She was so intent on getting the design exactly right that she didn't notice how late it was getting until Dad and Hank returned. Hank went right to the stove to warm up his hands, but Dad stopped, looking over Patsy's shoulder.

"See? I'm making hairbands that are zí, ská, and tȟó," Patsy said.

Dad's expression was a little surprised but mostly pleased.

"Those are beautiful," he said. "I can't wait to see you wear them."

Chapter 10

April 10, 1973

The next day, Patsy and Dad headed back to Pine Ridge to see if Pete had found the wire. This time, Hank got to come along. He spent the whole ride badgering Dad with questions about Denver and generators and shooting. Patsy wondered if her new little brother or sister would eventually be this talkative.

At Pete's service station, the newspapers in the rack had a disappointing headline.

April 10, 1973

WHITE HOUSE CANCELS MEETING WITH AIM
WOUNDED KNEE
OCCUPATION CONTINUES

Hopes for an end to the occupation of Wounded Knee were dashed over the weekend. American Indian Movement leader Russell Means came to Washington, DC, to meet with White House officials. The meeting was central to the agreement for ending the occupation. AIM hoped the White House would agree to launch investigations of past violations of treaties between the US government and various tribes. Additionally, AIM is seeking the removal of Oglala tribal president Dick Wilson. But the White House is refusing to meet with Means until the occupiers in Wounded Knee disarm. Means says government negotiators agreed the meeting would take place before any surrender. Further, Means says the occupiers will only disarm if the White House agrees to their demands. The standoff, now in its sixth week, will continue.

Pete appeared behind the counter as Dad and Patsy read the article.

"Just another example of white men lying to us," Pete said. "I don't know why AIM even bothers negotiating with these government guys. Or why any of our ancestors negotiated with them either. You can't trust a word they say."

"Maybe, but we've always been outnumbered and outgunned," Dad said. "If your choices are talking or dying, you might try talking. But I came in to talk about something else. You had any luck with that wire?"

"Yeah, man. I came through for you," Pete said.

"Thanks. That's great. How much do I owe you?"

"Don't worry about it. A cousin had it lying around out at his place. You know how we Lakota are. All we've got is nothing, but we're happy to share it. I left it in my car, though. Can you step outside with me?"

"Sure," Dad agreed.

"Hey, you kids want to pick a soda while we grab that wire? My treat," Pete offered.

Hank smiled broadly. "Yeah, thanks!"

Patsy nodded politely, but she had the feeling that Pete was trying to keep them out of the way. Dad and Pete headed outside while Hank debated between Coke and Fanta. What was Pete up to? Patsy slipped out the door and rounded the corner of the building. As she approached the lot behind the station, she heard Dad and Pete talking. She knew she wasn't supposed to eavesdrop, but she wanted to know what was going on.

"We need someone who knows the land and a truck that can go off-road. And from your place, it's under two miles to the drop location." It was Pete's voice.

"I don't know about this," Dad said. "I've got a kid to worry about. And another on the way. I don't want them growing up with their dad in jail. Or worse."

"There are kids out at Wounded Knee, even little babies and a couple of pregnant women. And they're hungry. The only food they're getting is what people are smuggling in on foot, and a backpack full of food doesn't go far for two hundred people. The government is trying to starve them out. I would deliver the food myself, but I think the FBI is watching me."

"Watching you? Why?" Dad asked.

"'Cause I'm a Lakota man with long hair who doesn't like Dick Wilson. Right now, that's enough to get the FBI on your tail."

"So, I wouldn't have to get into Wounded Knee. I'd just drop the food and supplies inside the government perimeter?"

"Yeah. From your place, you head north on the dirt road about a mile, then follow that ravine that runs northeast. It's less than a mile off-road. It's all marked on the map. Some people from AIM will hike out and pick it up."

"And where's all the stuff? How do I get it?" It sounded like Dad was agreeing.

"Someone will bring it to you before midnight tonight. You won't see them, and they won't see you. Safer for everyone that way. They'll drop it north of the highway, next to the dirt road leading to your place. That's on the map too."

"Okay. I'll do it," Dad said, "but I think I'd rather have just paid you for the wire."

Pete chuckled. Patsy hurried back inside before Dad or Pete spotted her. Hank was sipping an orange soda.

"Where'd you go?" he asked. "Do you want your soda?"

Patsy ignored his first question. "It's kind of cold for a soda today. You can have mine."

"Cool!" Hank said.

Dad returned, a spool of wire in hand. Patsy looked for a map, but if he had it with him, it was tucked out of sight.

"I'm going down to the pay phone on the corner to call Mom," he said, "to let her know I can fix the pump today and we'll be headed home tomorrow. Either of you want to come?"

Patsy wondered if he would tell her mom about smuggling food to Wounded Knee. She nodded.

"Sure," Hank said. "Can I say hi to Aunt Judy?"

Outside at the pay phone, with nothing to block the wind, Patsy shivered. Dad talked only for minute, explaining his plan to drive home the next day. He said nothing about the food for Wounded Knee. Then Hank got on. Patsy took one of his sodas so he could hold the receiver.

"Hey, Aunt Judy. Have you heard what's going on here?" he asked excitedly. "It's almost like a war. I've even heard some of the gunshots."

Patsy couldn't hear her mom's response, but she could guess.

"That's what my mom says too." Hank, looking deflated, handed the phone to Patsy. "I wish I were older."

"Hi, Pats." Mom's cheerful voice came through the receiver. "Are you having fun?"

"Definitely," Patsy said. But she felt a little guilty about keeping Dad's secret.

"I can't wait to see you tomorrow," Mom said. "I miss you both."

Patsy thought about seeing Mom in person the next day. She hoped Dad would tell her himself about smuggling the food. But if he didn't, could Patsy keep that secret? *Should* she keep that secret? She didn't want to hide things from her parents. Or for them to hide things from each other. "Miss you too."

"Well, I better hang up. Long distance is expensive. Love you."

"Love you too," Patsy said. "Bye, Mom."

~

After Dad put out the oil lamp that night, Patsy lay awake for what seemed like hours. Dad had fixed the pump. They'd had running water again by dinnertime. But he had said nothing to anyone about his plans for that night. Grandma, Aunt Marilyn, and Hank were all in the dark. Once, Patsy almost asked him about it. She tried to imagine what she'd say. But she wasn't sure if she wanted to talk him out of going or talk him into letting her come. Plus, she'd have to admit to eavesdropping.

From her cot next to the woodstove, Patsy listened for any sound coming from the couch where Dad slept. Or was he asleep? She couldn't hear the slow breathing that usually marked his slumber.

Finally, ever so quietly, Dad slipped from his blankets and sat on the edge of the couch. He must have kept his jeans and boots next to him. When he stood in the moonlight, he was dressed. He crossed the room to the door. It squeaked a bit as it opened. Patsy felt a hard lump rising in her throat. She was suddenly very scared for her dad. She was about to go after him when another figure came from the other room and followed him out the door. It was Aunt Marilyn, still in her nightgown. Patsy crept to the door.

Peeking through the window, Patsy saw they had stopped on the little porch. The door was still open a crack. For the second time that day, she eavesdropped.

"I'm not trying to stop you," Aunt Marilyn was saying. "I just want to know where you're going. Because if you're headed to Wounded Knee, Judy is going to kill us both."

"I'm only taking some food and medical supplies," Dad said. "I'm not even going into Wounded Knee. Just dropping them past the bunker, where the AIM guys can get to them."

"Maybe you should take the rifle," Aunt Marilyn said. At the mention of the rifle, the lump in Patsy's throat sunk to her stomach.

"Don't need a rifle, 'cause I'm not going to shoot anyone."

"But just in case."

"I figure an Indian who gets caught taking food to Wounded Knee is going to get off a lot easier than an Indian who gets caught taking a gun to Wounded Knee."

"You always were the smart one, Dan."

"Nah, that was you. That's why you fix people, and I only fix cars."

Suddenly, Patsy's worry turned into an idea. The truck was parked on the other side of the house. If she moved quickly, she could sneak out the door in the bedroom and be in the truck before her dad saw her.

There was no time to think. If she was going, she had to go now.

She pulled a flannel shirt over her pajamas and wrapped a blanket around her shoulders. Shoving her feet into her sneakers, she hoped Aunt Marilyn would keep Dad talking just a minute more.

When she was almost to the lean-to, a thought made Patsy spin around and return to the kitchen. The cracker tin was in the drawer, just where Grandma had left it. She grabbed the turtle charm and stuffed it into her shirt pocket. Seconds later, she was crawling into the back seat of the truck, pulling the door closed as quietly as she could. She lay down on the floor and covered herself with the dark blanket. With any luck, her dad wouldn't know she was there.

Patsy barely had enough time to take a breath before Dad climbed into the front seat. The key clicked, and the engine revved. The truck turned to head down the dirt road. With a minute to think, Patsy wondered exactly what she should do now. She was afraid Dad might get hurt, but what could she do to protect him? She decided she would stay put. They didn't have far to go. Maybe after the drop-off, she could sneak back into the house and Dad would

never know. Or maybe he'd find her, and she'd have to come clean. She would cross that bridge when she had to. She pulled the turtle charm from her pocket and squeezed it. Keya was a survivor.

Soon Dad parked the truck and got out. Patsy heard the clunk of the tailgate and the rasp of cardboard boxes sliding across the bed. He had found the supplies. The first part of the plan had worked.

When they were moving again, Patsy tried to guess how much time was passing and how fast they were moving. They had perhaps two miles to backtrack up the dirt road and then another mile to get to the ravine. The truck was loaded down, and the dirt road was bumpy. They were going slowly, maybe twenty miles per hour. She realized this was a math problem. Somehow, that calmed her racing heart. Patsy imagined the numbers written in a notebook, just like any other homework problem. At that speed, it would take them about nine minutes on the road. Hadn't it been almost that long already?

Patsy began counting the seconds. It was something for her mind to do besides worry. A couple of minutes later, she felt the truck lurch through a ditch. They must be off the road now. Dad slowed the truck. According to Pete, it was less than a mile cross-country. She guessed they were going half as fast as before. She saw the numbers in her mind. At this speed, it would be six minutes at the most to the drop site. Six minutes times sixty seconds per minute was 360.

Patsy started her counting again at one. She was only at 324 when the truck slowed and stopped. Dad began unloading. So far, so good. Patsy dared to peek from under the blanket. She raised her head just enough to see boxes stacked against the back window. That meant Dad couldn't see her. Rising to her knees, she peered through the windshield.

Maybe half a mile away, the district of Wounded Knee lay quiet. Most of it was blanketed in shadow, but a white church gleamed atop a little hill. It was the church she had seen in the news. Patsy knew protesters would be sleeping inside that church tonight. Nearby, a small white triangle pointed up toward the moon. It was the tipi, standing like a steeple on ground. And right next to the church lay hundreds of Lakota, buried for more than eighty years.

CRACK!

Patsy screamed. That was a gunshot.

Chapter 11

April 10, 1973

Crack! Crack!

Two more shots rang out.

"Oof," Dad groaned behind the truck.

Patsy threw off the blanket. The shots sounded like they were coming from a rise out the driver's side. Keeping low, she jumped out the passenger-side door. Dad sat against the back tire, holding his left arm.

"Patsy?" Dad's eyes were wide as quarters. "What in the name of creation are you doing here?"

"We've got to get out of here," Patsy said, ignoring his question. "Someone is shooting at us!"

Crack! A fourth shot kicked up dirt behind the truck.

"Get in the truck!" Dad yelled.

Patsy grabbed Dad's arm. He yelped in pain.

"Did you get shot?"

"They got my arm, but I can walk. Get in the truck!"

As Patsy and Dad scrambled into the cab, a bullet hit the bed.

"I can hardly lift my arm," Dad said. His sleeve was torn. Below his left elbow, the fabric was soaked in blood. Patsy's stomach churned as she looked at the dark stains.

"I can work the pedals and shift gears, but you'll have to take the wheel," he said.

The engine hummed, and Dad put it in gear. Patsy took a deep breath and scooted as close to him as she could. She gripped the steering wheel in both hands.

"We've got to make a U-turn. Cut it to the right as far as it can go."

Patsy jerked the wheel hard, and her dad gave the car some gas.

Crack!

Another shot whistled past the windshield. Patsy flinched but kept both hands on the wheel. The truck

lurched forward. Rocks crunched beneath the tires as they made a tight turn.

"Now straighten out," Dad said.

Patsy let the wheel slide back to the left, and her dad nodded.

"Good," he said. "Hold it steady. We're going to follow along the bottom of the ravine. Just keep it in the middle."

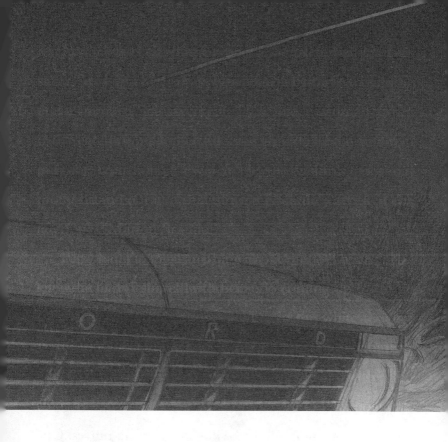

Patsy's fingers were white from clinging to the wheel, but she did what Dad said.

"What if they follow us? What will we do?" Patsy tried not to sound as scared as she felt.

"Just focus on driving," Dad said. "I don't see anyone behind us."

Patsy glanced behind and saw no one. But as she turned her head back, she saw the muscles pulled tight along Dad's jaw. Beads of sweat covered his forehead.

"We need to do something about your arm," Patsy said.

"When we're in the clear," Dad said. "Just keep your eyes on the ground. It curves left here. Good. Now straight again."

With Dad guiding her, Patsy steered them back to the road.

"We better stop here," Dad said. "I want to make sure no one is following us before we go home."

"Home? What about your arm? We need to go to the hospital!"

"That hospital is full of white doctors and nurses. One of them might think it's their civic duty to turn in a Lakota man who got shot smuggling food into Wounded Knee."

"But you can hardly move your arm," Patsy protested.

"I think the bullet passed through. Didn't hit the bone. Marilyn can look at it. She'll know if it's serious."

"We should at least try to stop the bleeding," Patsy said. "If you pass out, we'll both be stuck out here."

"You got a point there," Dad said. Using his right hand, he pulled a pocketknife from his jeans and handed it to Patsy. "Use that to cut a slit near the edge of your blanket. Then rip a strip off."

Patsy cut the edge, then pulled hard. After a couple more yanks, a strip came away. Dad turned his arm toward her.

"Now wrap that as tight as you can," said Dad. "Leave the two ends free so we can tie them up."

"Got it," Patsy said, but her hands trembled as she lifted the bit of blanket.

"You're doing great. I'm really proud of you, my Brave Bird."

Patsy wrapped the cloth around Dad's arm a couple of times, then tugged to knot the ends. Dad gave a little snort and gritted his teeth. With the knot secured, they checked the shadowy landscape.

"I don't see anyone behind us," Dad said. "I think we can head back. You got the wheel for another mile?"

Patsy nodded.

"I'll take it slow. Just stay in the middle of the road."

Driving on the road was easier, but Patsy still sighed with relief when she could finally let go of the wheel. Aunt Marilyn must have been watching for them. She came out of the house before Dad had the truck in park. When she saw Patsy in the front seat, she looked mad enough to spit. She yanked the door open and stood with both hands on her hips.

"Patricia Brave Bird Antoine, what are you doing in that truck? And here I've been keeping quiet trying not to wake you up." Aunt Marilyn had used Patsy's full name. She was in trouble. Luckily, Dad saved her from explaining.

"That discussion will have to wait, Marilyn," he said. "I need your professional services."

Patsy hopped out of the truck, and Aunt Marilyn got a look at Dad's arm.

"Did you get yourself shot?" she demanded.

"Just a little scratch," Dad said.

"Who was shooting at you?"

"Don't know," he said. "They were hidden behind a ridge. But I didn't see a car, and they didn't follow us. So probably not marshals or FBI. Maybe some goons. Could even have been an AIM patrol that didn't get the word to expect me."

"We should take you to the hospital."

"I was hoping you'd take a look first. I'm guessing there might be a white doctor or two who would be happy to inform the FBI about a guy showing up with a suspicious gunshot wound."

Sighing, Aunt Marilyn ran a hand through her long hair. "We better get both of you inside. I'll see what I can do. You're not the first Indian to show up here in the middle of the night because he was afraid to see a white doctor."

Dad eased himself out of the truck and leaned against Marilyn's shoulder.

"Like I said, Judy is going to kill us both," she said.

"About Judy," said Dad. "Someone is going to have to go into town tomorrow to call and tell her what's going on. And right now, I can't drive."

"Then I'll drive you," Marilyn said. "But you're doing the talking."

"Dad, will you tell Mom about me hiding in the truck?" Patsy asked.

"Patsy, you were so brave tonight. And if you hadn't been there, I might have been stuck out in that ravine."

At Dad's words, Patsy felt her stomach unknot for the first time since she'd left the house. She had been brave when she most needed to be. And they'd made it home. But she sensed a *but* was coming.

"But stowing away like that was dangerous. And there will be consequences. So yes, I'm telling your mother. But don't worry too much." He winked. "By the time she's finished with me, she'll probably have blown off most of her steam."

Patsy swallowed, wondering what those consequences might be. Still, if she could go back, she wouldn't do anything differently. Except for a single box, all the supplies had been dropped off. Maybe the occupiers would still get them. And she had helped her dad when he might have been stranded, or worse. After following Dad and Aunt Marilyn into the house, Patsy tucked the keya charm safely back into its tin.

April 10, 1973

Dad is finally asleep. Aunt Marilyn said he was lucky. The bullet passed through his arm without hitting the bone or an artery. Keya did its job. Aunt Marilyn cleaned the wound and put a few stitches in it. I couldn't watch her, but I watched Dad's face. He was sweating and clenching his jaw the whole time. Hank and Grandma woke up when they heard us come in. When he heard the story, Hank was jealous that he had missed it. He even went out and found the bullet hole in the truck. I think he's a little mad at me for not bringing him along. Aunt Marilyn put some dried ground yarrow on the wound to prevent an infection. She will try to get some antibiotics at the hospital tomorrow too. Dad was exhausted, but he still tossed and turned for a long time. Probably from the pain.

It will be dawn soon, but I can't sleep. Every time I close my eyes, I think I hear distant gunshots. Maybe it's just my imagination.

Or maybe whoever was shooting at us found a new target. My heart has stopped racing, but I feel more afraid than I did back in that ravine. Dad could have been killed tonight. I could have been killed. And there are still a couple hundred people inside Wounded Knee, even little kids and babies. They could be killed. No one has died so far. But will that luck hold out? And when this is all done and the FBI and marshals leave, will Wilson and his goons still be here?

In some ways, I can't wait to get home and feel safe again. But I feel guilty leaving Grandma, Aunt Marilyn, and Hank while this is still going on.

Chapter 12

April 11–18, 1973

Dear Laura,
My dad hurt his arm in an accident, so we're
staying another week or so. I'll miss a couple of
days of school. Will you help me catch up, please?
And I'm grounded for the rest of the trip. I can't
go farther than the outhouse. I'll tell you why
when I get back. It's not so bad, though. I'm
having fun with my family. My grandma is also
helping me make a couple of things, including
something for you!

Your friend, Patsy

April 11, 1973

Laura O'Sullivan
825 Liman St.
Denver, CO
80204

It had been almost a week since the shooting. Dad's arm was better. At least, he thought, better enough to drive. They would leave the next morning. Basket in hand, Patsy headed to the chicken coop to collect eggs when the *pop* of Hank's BB gun startled her. Was Hank shooting the chickens?

Pop! Pop! Pop!

The gun fired again and again. Rounding the corner of the house, Patsy saw the coop. It wasn't Hank. A man in dark clothes was shooting into the coop. And the gun looked real. The chickens squawked and flapped, trying to escape.

"Stop!" Patsy shouted.

The man turned, but a hood shadowed his face. She couldn't tell who it was. He took aim at her. She tried to run, but she couldn't move. Her brain told her legs to run, but she was stuck fast to the ground.

Pop!

Patsy screamed. A hand grabbed her shoulder.

"Pit-a-pat," Dad whispered in her ear. "Wake up. You're dreaming. It's okay."

Patsy opened her eyes. In the dark, she could just make out Dad's face a few inches away.

"It was a dream. You're safe," Dad said.

Had that just been a dream? It seemed so real.

Pop.

Patsy shuddered. That sound was real. It was muffled and distant, but real.

Dad wrapped his good arm around her shoulder. "It's gunfire, but it's far away. Out at Wounded Knee. You're safe here."

Patsy pressed her face into Dad's shoulder. She nodded but held on tight to his neck for a long time.

"It's still the middle of the night," Dad said. "Try to go back to sleep."

Patsy's heart juddered in her chest. "I don't think I can sleep."

"Let's pull your cot over by the couch," Dad said. "I'll be right beside you."

Patsy felt better next to her dad, but she still lay awake a long time. It seemed she had just dozed off when a new sound, this one like an angry bee, woke her. Dad sat up.

"What's that?" Patsy asked.

"Sounds like a plane," Dad said.

The bedroom door opened, and Aunt Marilyn, Hank, and Grandma all shuffled out in their pajamas. The noise was getting louder.

Aunt Marilyn pulled back the window curtain. Dawn had begun to paint the sky pink.

"It is a plane," she said. "No, wait—it's three planes."

"Can I go see, please?" Hank begged. He wasn't going to miss out on any excitement this time.

Aunt Marilyn nodded, folding him in a blanket. Grabbing the remaining covers from the couch and cot, the rest of the family followed Hank outside.

The three small planes were coming from the west. In less than a minute, they had passed over, heading on to Wounded Knee. A dark bundle dropped from the first plane. And then a second bundle. A brilliant red parachute opened above the second bundle, but the parachute on the first trailed it like a kite tail. The lead plane banked right as two bundles dropped from the second plane, then two more from the third. Their chutes mushroomed

open and, glowing in the rosy dawn, floated down into Wounded Knee. The first plane finished circling around and made another pass overhead. Two more bundles, with parachutes spread wide, landed in the district. Then the planes disappeared into the rising sun.

"That was so cool!" Hank said. "What do you think is in those bags? Guns?"

"I doubt it," Dad said. "Probably food. Someone doesn't want the protesters to get starved out—someone with a lot of guts and enough money to get a hold of three airplanes."

"Probably not an Indian then," Grandma said. "I know plenty of Indians with a lot of guts. But I don't know any with that much money."

"It's nice to think the people in Wounded Knee aren't alone," Patsy said. "They have friends who want to help."

"I don't think I can go back to sleep after that," Aunt Marilyn said. "Anyone else ready for breakfast?"

~

All morning, if they were quiet, the family heard the *pop* of distant gunshots. Patsy wished they could turn on a

TV or radio to cover up the sound. How long could this go on without someone getting hurt?

Aunt Marilyn went to work, and Dad went into town to fill the truck and the gas cans for the generator. He took Hank, but Patsy couldn't go because she was still grounded—the consequences Dad had promised. Patsy didn't mind. After her nearly sleepless night, she was tired. She tried to take a nap, but the gunfire kept her awake. From this distance, it wasn't loud. But each shot made her think about the danger facing everyone on the reservation, including her family. Finally, she gave up on napping and joined Grandma, who was finishing the repairs on the cradleboard.

"Grandma, maybe you and Aunt Marilyn and Hank should come to Denver with us," Patsy said. "At least for a little while, until all this trouble ends."

Grandma smiled but shook her head. "I'm glad you want us, but my home is here. Marilyn feels the same way. The work she does at the hospital is important. They need more Native doctors and nurses. Not fewer."

"I'm worried about you. Even if the occupation ends soon, Wilson and his goons will still be here."

Grandma squeezed Patsy's hand. "There are troubles anywhere you go, Patsy. Sometimes I think we Lakota have had more than our share. But we are survivors. We'll get through this."

"Then maybe Dad and I should stay longer," Patsy said.

"Your home is in Denver. Indians lived all over this country before white people came. There's no reason they shouldn't live in every part of the country now. And what your dad and mom are doing there is important too. When they decided to get married, they knew troubles would come, for them and for their kids. So, remember you are Lakota, and you are a survivor."

"Like keya," Patsy said.

"Exactly. Like keya." Grandma smiled. "But come back and see us soon. And bring your mother and the baby. Babies are a gift for the whole tiyóspaye."

Patsy was about to reply, but she heard a new sound, and it was getting louder.

"Is that another plane?" Patsy wondered.

"Come on," Grandma said.

For the second time that day, they went outside and studied the sky. A helicopter flew toward them from the north. As they stood shading their eyes, Dad and Hank pulled into the driveway. They hopped out of the truck and joined Patsy and Grandma, watching the helicopter approach then land just south of Wounded Knee.

"Maybe this is guns!" Hank said.

Dad shook his head. "It's pretty far away, but that looks like a government helicopter. My guess is someone got hurt and they're taking them to a hospital."

"I hope whoever it is will be okay," Patsy said.

But if they were bringing in a helicopter, she knew it had to be serious. She thought about what Dad had said about it taking a martyr to get people's attention. The protesters at Wounded Knee wouldn't still be there unless they were willing to risk their lives. Even Dad had been willing to take a big risk. He had been lucky. Would they?

April 18, 1973

We said goodbye to our South Dakota family this morning. Before we left, Grandma handed me a little paper bag. "For the baby," she said. The keya charm was inside. I will make sure it goes in the crib. I am anxious to get home, but I feel like I am leaving a piece of my heart behind.

I could tell Dad's arm was hurting by the time we got to the Colorado border. But he said he was okay, and we made it. Mom was so relieved, she was crying. I didn't even mind that she called me Pit-a-pat. When she hugged me, she didn't let go for a long time. She had some good news too. The loan for the house has been approved! We will move next month.

I go back to school tomorrow. Even though I've been gone less than two weeks, it seems much longer. Like things are different somehow. Or maybe like I'm different somehow. It wasn't the spring break I was expecting, but I'm so glad I went.

Chapter 13

May 2–12, 1973

*P*atsy took a deep breath as she faced her classmates. It was her turn for current events day. Everyone looked up at her from their desks. Actually, a couple of kids were looking out the window, and one was tying his shoe, but a lot of faces stared at her. She glanced at Laura. They were both wearing their new hairbands. Laura smiled her encouragement. Patsy tried to ignore the jumpy feeling in her stomach.

"Today, instead of reading a newspaper article, Miss Ashman said I could read a letter from my aunt," Patsy said. "My aunt is Lakota. She lives on the Pine Ridge Indian Reservation just a couple miles from Wounded

Knee. I went to visit her and my grandmother and cousin during spring break. Early in the morning, the day before we left, we heard gunfire. Then at dawn, we saw three airplanes use parachutes to drop food into Wounded Knee. That same afternoon, a helicopter landed. We thought it was taking someone to a hospital."

"Wow," Carlos said. "I went to my grandma's for spring break, but all I did was watch game shows on TV."

Miss Ashman raised her eyebrows at Carlos. "Please continue, Patricia," she said.

"After we came home, my aunt sent this letter."

April 28, 1973
Dear Tiyóspaye,

You were right about the planes that dropped the food. The airlift was organized by an activist from Boston. And he is white and a pilot. You were right about the helicopter too. One of the occupiers, a guy named Frank Clearwater, was shot in the head. The helicopter took him to a hospital in Rapid City. But he didn't make it. He died three days ago.

Sadly, another person died yesterday. And this time it was a Lakota man and someone we knew—Buddy Lamont. I was working when they brought his body into the hospital. I talked to his mother, Agnes. He was shot in the back. She thinks a government sniper got him. But there are rumors that someone from AIM shot him to get more sympathy for their cause. Agnes wants to bury her son in the cemetery at Wounded Knee, next to the grave site from the massacre. Dick Wilson is trying to block it. I hope she'll get her way, though. It seems the only fitting place.

After these two deaths, both sides seem more anxious to reach an agreement. I just hope it will accomplish something. AIM hopes to get rid of Dick Wilson, protect our civil rights, and restore our treaty rights. If even one of those things happens, then maybe this will have been worth it.

Thečhíȟila,
Marilyn

Patsy folded the letter and glanced at Miss Ashman.

Miss Ashman nodded her approval, then turned to the class. "Any comments or questions?"

Carlos raised his hand, and Miss Ashman pointed to him.

"Did you know that Lakota man who got killed?" Carlos asked.

"Buddy Lamont? No, but my dad did," Patsy said. "And I met his mother during our trip. It's sad and strange to think that her son was shot just a couple weeks later."

"What does your aunt mean by civil rights and treaty rights?" Carlos asked next.

"The Lakota and other Native American people want to be treated fairly. They want the federal government to honor their treaties. They want tribal governments that protect their land and people. They want respect for their traditions and culture. They want the police to protect them and not harass them just because they're Indians."

"If your aunt is Lakota, does that mean you're Lakota too?" Frank asked.

"Yes," Patsy said. "My father is Lakota. That makes me Lakota."

"Are you going to join AIM? 'Cause my dad says they're Communists," said Frank.

Laura slapped her forehead at Frank's comment. Patsy almost giggled.

"First of all, the people in AIM aren't Communists. I still don't think I'll join AIM, though." Patsy remembered that night in the ravine. She didn't think guns would solve their problems. "But there are other ways to stand up for our people."

"Like what?" Donna asked.

"Well, I'm learning Lakota. And I'm telling all of you about what's happening at Wounded Knee. That's a beginning."

"It's a good beginning. Thank you, Patricia," said Miss Ashman. "And now it's time to move on to today's lesson. Everyone, please take out your books and open to page 165."

Laura flashed Patsy a thumbs-up. Back at her desk, Patsy tucked away her aunt's letter.

"Hey, Patsy, you know how your middle name is Brave Bird?" Laura whispered as their classmates turned pages.

Patsy nodded.

"It suits you."

May 12, 1973

We moved into our new house today! It took half a dozen trips with the truck loaded to get everything here. The ash tree has leafed out. We were glad for the shade as we carried everything in. It felt like summer today. Most things are still in boxes, including all the pots and pans. Mom and Dad splurged on pizza for dinner. We got the beds set up, so we all have a place to sleep tonight.

Dad said while he had the tools out, he might as well put up the crib. I tied the keya charm to one of the slats. The baby will know she is Lakota and a survivor. Or he. A boy would be okay too. With the occupation over, Mom says we can go back to South Dakota this summer, after the baby comes. Our tiyóspaye will be all together.

The occupation of Wounded Knee ended four days ago. The occupiers agreed to disarm. Some of them will be charged with crimes. But Dad says there are good lawyers who support their cause who will defend them. The federal government agreed to investigate Dick Wilson and the tribal government. They will also send White House officials to South Dakota to discuss treaty violations.

I wonder what will happen after that. I asked Dad if he thought the Lakota would get the Black Hills back. "Not likely," was all he said. But I think some good has to come from all this. Native people talked about the broken treaties and massacres of the past with millions of people listening. They also talked about the unfair ways Indians are treated today. Even movie stars far away in Hollywood and a pilot in Boston were listening and wanted to help. And members of tribes from all over the country worked together both inside and outside Wounded Knee. Those are all good things.

I still like math better than social studies, but I understand now what Miss Ashman said about thinking about what you think. The questions with no easy answers can be the most important ones to ask.

Author's Note

This book is fictional. Patsy, her family, and their experiences are the inventions of my imagination. However, the events of the Wounded Knee protest really did happen. Also, several people mentioned in the book were real people: Dr. Martin Luther King Jr., Richard Nixon, Russell Means, Richard (Dick) Wilson, Marlon Brando, Sacheen Littlefeather, Frank Clearwater, Lawrence (Buddy) Lamont, and Agnes Lamont. Buddy Lamont was buried next to the Wounded Knee grave site. When Agnes died in 1982, she was too. The pilot who organized the airlift of food was William (Bill) Zimmerman.

The year 1973 is recent enough that I was lucky to have many excellent sources: newspapers from the time, accounts written by both occupiers and government officials, books by historians and scholars, and sound recordings and videos made during and soon after the occupation. You can even watch Sacheen Littlefeather's Oscars speech on YouTube. The source that proved to be the most valuable was *Voices from Wounded Knee, 1973: In the Words of Participants*. Published in 1974, the book includes journal entries, interviews, poems, songs, press conferences, maps, photographs, and even radio conversations between government officials and protesters.

During the 1970s, American Indian Movement leaders were criticized for using violence. A Black activist named Ray Robinson disappeared from Wounded Knee during the protest. Afterward, witnesses said that AIM leaders killed Robinson. Some said AIM thought Robinson was spying for the FBI. Others said he got in an argument with AIM's leaders. Several witnesses have also said that AIM leaders ordered the murder of Anna Mae Aquash three years later. Aquash had been part of the occupation. AIM leaders later suspected her of spying for the FBI.

Since then, AIM has turned to peaceful methods. They have supported Native American schools, a housing project in Minneapolis, Native American media, and educational and cultural programs. In 2020, unarmed members of AIM patrolled Native American neighborhoods in Minneapolis during the uprising after police murdered George Floyd.

Like Pete does in the book, you might say the story of the 1973 protest began with the murder of Wesley Bad

Heart Bull in January 1973. Or, like Aunt Marilyn, you could say it started when Dick Wilson became president of the tribe in 1972. Taking a wider view, you could trace its beginning to the termination policies of the 1950s and '60s, which tried to force Native nations to disappear into the broader American culture. Or you might point to laws from the 1800s that took tribal lands and outlawed Native religions and practices. You could also start at the 1890 massacre or the violations of the 1868 treaty. But, in many ways, this story began when the first European colonists arrived in North America in the fifteenth century.

Likewise, it is hard to say when the story of Wounded Knee ended. Maybe it hasn't ended. I wish I could report that the protest restored treaty rights and ended the unfair treatment of Native Americans. Or that Dick Wilson was removed from office, and prosperity came to the Pine Ridge Indian Reservation. But none of those things happened.

Dick Wilson stayed in office for three more years. During that time, dozens of Wilson's critics were killed. In fact, the Pine Ridge Indian Reservation had the highest rate of murder of anywhere in the United States. Indigenous

Americans on Pine Ridge and elsewhere continued to face discrimination, poverty, and harassment. In many cases, they still do.

Treaty rights have never been fully restored, but some progress has been made. Native nations have regained more of their rights to govern themselves, practice their religions, and manage their land. Also, in 1980, the US Supreme Court said the US government had illegally taken the Black Hills from the Lakota people. The government was ordered to pay the Lakota $117 million. But the Lakota didn't want the money. They wanted the Black Hills. Since then, the money has been sitting in an account earning interest. The account is now worth more than one billion dollars.

Many impacts of the protest continue. Along with other events of the 1960s and '70s, it brought attention to the injustice Native people had suffered and continued to face. It helped Indigenous Americans feel proud of their heritage. It helped nations want to preserve their traditions, languages, and religions. It led to more cooperation between different nations. Also, some Native Americans became friends with Black Americans and Latinx Americans who were also fighting for their civil rights.

The story of Wounded Knee is dramatic and important. Both of those qualities make it a great setting for a novel. And the South Dakota landscape lends itself to adventure. But mostly, I wanted to tell a story about Wounded Knee because I have child who, like Patsy, is half Lakota. I hope that he will also find his own way to proudly be Lakota.

An AIM poster calls for support and an immediate cease-fire.

Five years after the 1973 Wounded Knee occupation, AIM led the Longest Walk, a peaceful protest in which supporters walked from San Francisco to Washington, DC, to bring attention to legislation that would threaten Native American lands and rights. None of the bills they protested were passed.

About the Author

Rachel Bithell writes about history, culture, and science for kids and their caregivers. Her writing has been featured in several national magazines. This is her first book. As a foster and adoptive parent and former teacher, she has cared for and taught many children with diverse strengths, interests, backgrounds, and needs. For all these children, storytelling has served her as an invaluable tool for connecting and learning.

About the Illustrator

Eric Freeberg has illustrated over twenty-five books for children and has created work for magazines and ad campaigns. He was a winner of the 2010 London Book Fair's Children's Illustration Competition; the 2010 Holbein Prize for Fantasy Art, International Illustration Competition, Japan Illustrators' Association; Runner-Up, 2013 SCBWI Magazine Merit Award; Honorable Mention, 2009 SCBWI Don Freeman Portfolio Competition; and 2nd Prize, 2009 Clymer Museum's Annual Illustration Invitational. He was also a winner of the Elizabeth Greenshields Foundation Award.

History is full of storytellers

**Take a sneak peek at an excerpt from
*If the Fire Comes: A Story of Segregation during the
Great Depression* by Tracy Daley, another story from
the I Am America series.**

———————◆———————

August 5, 1935
Mission: Save the Pigeons
Operative: Joseph McCoy

Summary:

It's been a week since I brought the pigeons home.
They made Maya smile. The last few months since
she's had polio have been hard. Her legs don't work
right anymore, and she's been stuck in bed. There
are two things that cheer her up: my spy stories
and the presents I bring home—the pigeons being
the best find so far.

      I tell her the story every night to see if she'll
smile again—how I knew the gambler, a pigeon

racer, was down on his luck. I'd shined his shoes a dozen times, so I'd heard all his stories. I followed him five blocks without being noticed, sly as a real spy, and watched him dump his losing birds in the trash behind the mercantile.

Maya's favorite part is how I waited until he left and then saved the birds, bent cages and all.

I'd heard how pigeons can send messages, and I thought Maya and I could use them in our spy games, but something's wrong. The last few days, the pigeons have been lying down, not getting up when I bring them the leftover cornbread and milk. Maya says they are sick because we aren't feeding them right.

Today, I'm going to make enough money to get real pigeon feed. I might have to shine a dozen shoes to do it, but I'm not coming home until I can make the birds better. I worry that if something happens to the pigeons, Maya might never smile again.

*J*oseph McCoy could tell a lot by the shoes a person wore. Or didn't wear.

Uncle Tanner's shoes sat by the door of the shop Joseph and his family lived in, untouched on a weekday morning. Uncle Tanner's boots, a pair of Red Wings worn down to the metal over the toe, told the story of a man who'd worked hard once.

Shifting the boots to set his shoeshine box down by the door, Joseph could smell the oil and smoke from the leather. Uncle Tanner had been a metalworker before the Depression. He'd even been able to save up to have his own shop and tools, but he'd been out of work for almost two years now. His boots sat by the door more and more often. It was rare for Uncle Tanner to even come out of the back room now.

Joseph checked his shoeshine box, making sure his supplies were ready for the day: black liquid, polishing cloth, Griffin shoe polish, and several small brushes. Joseph was the best shoeshine in Elsinore, California. He knew how to get every detail right, and his hands didn't shake, steady and sure. He never got black on a customer's socks. Joseph could tell the difference between a movie star and an athlete, a businessman and a crook, or a banker and a lawyer.

"You leaving already?" Maya asked, making Joseph jump.

"I want to get an early start," Joseph said, walking across the shop to the side of Maya's bed. She slept out in the open; Joseph slept on the floor next to her. The shop only had one room in the back, where Uncle Tanner disappeared to more and more often.

Maya was two years older than Joseph, a ripe old age of thirteen, but she still liked to play their spy game. And even though she didn't get around the way she used to, she could talk all day, fix a clock without thinking, and pinch as hard as a crab.

Joseph was about to sit down next to her when he heard cooing coming from Maya's feet. Not again. He pulled the thin blanket up from the bottom and found Simon, Maya's favorite bird. He was nestled between

Maya's crooked legs, thin as pencils. He could see a spot of blood on her ankles from where she must have dragged her legs across the floor.

"Simon wasn't feeling well. I wanted to keep him warm," Maya said, sticking her chin out in her stubborn way.

"Are you okay?" Joseph asked.

"Of course," Maya said, but Joseph saw her tuck her hands behind her back. She got slivers when she dragged herself across the shop, no matter how many times Joseph swept. Maya was hard to keep down.

Want to read what happens next?

Check out
If the Fire Comes:
A Story of Segregation during the Great Depression